W9-DGO-492

Asian Tales and Tellers

Asian Tales and Tellers

Cathy Spagnoli

August House Publishers Inc.
LITTLE ROCK

Published 1998 by August House, Inc.,
P.O. Box 3223, Little Rock, Arkansas, 72203,
501-372-5450.

Printed in the United States of America
10 9 8 7 6 5 4 3 2 1

LIBRARY OF CONGRESS CATALOGING-IN-PUBLICATION DATA
Spagnoli, Cathy.
Asian tales and tellers / Cathy Spagnoli.
p. cm.
Includes bibliographical references.
ISBN 0-87483-527-5 (hbk.)—ISBN 0-87483-526-7 (pbk.)
1. Tales—Asia. 2. Tales—Asia, Southeastern. 3. Folklore—Japan. 4. Folklore—China. 5. Folklore—Southeast Asia. 6. Story telling—Asia. 7. Story telling—Asia, Southeastern.
I. Title.
GR265.S63 1998
398.2'095—dc21 98-29930

Executive editor: Liz Parkhurst
Project editor: Tom Baskett, Jr.
Cover design: Wendell E. Hall
Interior drawings: Paramasivam Samanna
Book design: Shirley Brainard

For permission to quote from their publications, the following are gratefully acknowledged: *Appleseed Quarterly* for Kate Stevens's "The World of the Chinese Storyteller," vol. 7 (Spring 1997): 17-23; and Westview Press, Boulder, Colorado, for Shigeru Kayano's *Our Land Was a Forest*, translated by Kyoko Selden and Lily Selden, 1994.

AUGUST HOUSE, INC. PUBLISHERS LITTLE ROCK

For Gene Spagnoli,
who so richly loved and lived;
for Harriet Hanke Spagnoli,
who so truly give and inspires;
and, always, for Sivam and Manu.

Contents

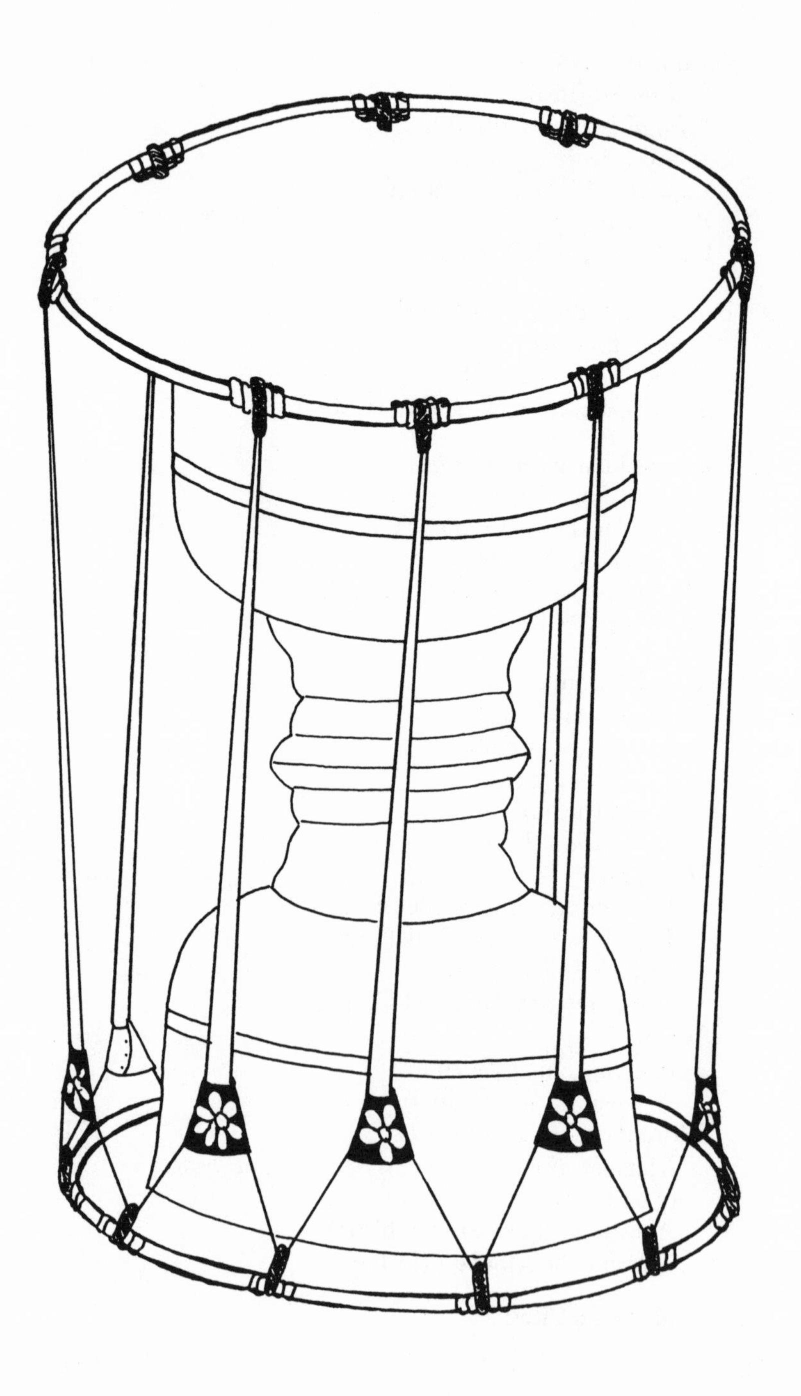

ACKNOWLEDGMENTS

Since my knowledge of Asia and Asian storytelling is limited, I asked those who knew more about certain cultures to help out, and they have been most generous. I credit their stories and comments in the book and thank them here as well: Kate Stevens, Patrick Harrigan, Wajuppa Tossa, Margaret Read MacDonald, Shigeru Kayano, Jeff Tsay, Joanna C. Yu, and A.D. Edward Raj.

Countless kind people have helped me to learn about stories in my travels and projects here and abroad. I wish I could list them all. Any who shared tales so willingly are credited in the notes.

Others have done more than their fair share to teach me about Asia and its stories over the years. To them goes the credit for the best of this book. All the mistakes are mine alone, with the solace of Confucius: *Our greatest glory is not in never falling, but in rising every time we fall.* I specifically want to thank my family and Yukiko Kusumoto; warm friends in Cholamandal, Banyan Teacher Centre, Dakshina Chitra and INTACH in India; great folks at Vashon Library and King County Interlibrary Loan; The Korea Foundation and The Korea Society; and The Japan Foundation and Hyogo Cultural Center.

Heartfelt gratitude goes as well to Yong Jin Choi, Yong-hi and In-hak Choi, Kyoko Matsuoka, Koji and Kazuko Inada, Dharampal, Ram Swarup, Indira Seshagiri Rao, Yutaka Hotta, Tae Kyun Kim, Keiichi Hatanaka, Thom Kong, Tsutsui Etsuko, Lina Mao Wall, Ukawa family, Chinna Oommen, Toshio Abe, Sachiko and Chie Yokoyama, Emanuelle Chi Dang, Akemi Yagi, Mary Hammond Bernson, Young Sook and Young Ok Song, Keiko Shirane, Blia Xiong, Kazuko Sugimoto, K.G. Rastogi, Putha Touch, Kazuko Matsuura, Maxine Loo, Noto Storytellers, and Refugee Women's Alliance.

Finally, a special "hooray" for those who turned these tales into a book: Liz Parkhurst, who combines compassion, skill, and enthusiasm; Tom Baskett, Jr., who edits with sharp eyes and understanding; and all the talented people at August House.

PREFACE

Jasmine scented the air as my friend Saraswati took Manu, my toddler son, off to play. I started telling stories to about six hundred students sitting near the huge banyan tree in a peaceful Indian schoolyard. Halfway through my telling, though, the quiet was broken by my son's shouts. I told on, knowing Saraswati was with him. Yet his cries came closer and closer, full of loss and hunger. I spoke a few more words; then suddenly he was right behind me, sobbing in desperation. Picking him up, I ended the story, struggling to be heard as Manu screamed into the microphone.

Ready to begin another tale, I hugged him, then gently tried to return him to Saraswati. He clung only to me. A friendly teacher came to help, but Manu clutched me and ignored her. Next, children were sent up with candy, yet even that didn't tempt him away! I was upset, torn—I had a program to finish as well as a son to soothe. As I stood there, about to cry myself, the principal spoke from the back, where he sat with visiting dignitaries from nearby towns.

"Your child needs you now," he said. "Of course, we want to hear your tales. But we have time. We can wait. Go and take care of him. We'll be here." And so I went to the girls' hostel and after ten minutes, Manu was sleeping with a smile. I returned to find everyone waiting patiently. We shared a wonderful time of telling, and I realized again how much I could learn from India.

Since 1970, I've lived, worked, and shared stories for over twelve years in India, Japan, Korea, and parts of South Asia. Here in Washington state, I have exchanged tales with gracious Southeast Asian refugees. As I met with Asian tellers, scholars, and listeners here and abroad, I often asked, "What stories would you like Americans to hear? Why?" Some of the answers and the tales I received make up this book.

In the following pages are tales from that part of Asia extending from Pakistan across to Japan. I have tried to represent most of this region through story, although the selection obviously reflects my own travels and collecting. Bundling together such diverse nations is both simplistic and perhaps confusing, yet it seemed possible to present these stories as a friend sharing gifts given, and to hope that you will make further explorations on your own.

The book begins with a very brief look at Asia, the setting. The first two chapters then introduce several modern Asian storytellers and styles, to provide a living cultural context for the tales and to offer ideas that may be useful for your work as storyteller, teacher, student, librarian, or global citizen.

Stories follow, grouped under themes suggested by Asian and Asian American friends. The selections cover the range of a storytelling repertoire (except the epics), and include folk tales, true stories, legends, verse, and jokes. Most are tales I heard in my work (often with the help of kind interpreters); some I gleaned through book research; almost all I have told.

They are written to be read or told, although they are not written exactly as I heard them for I am a storyteller, not a folklore scholar. I sought stories wherever and whenever I could, and thus frequently had to rely upon my notes and my friends to reconstruct the tales. Many times a story came to me from someone who was not a practiced teller, who gave the tale in bits and pieces which I later put together after careful cultural research.

Brief introductions begin each story chapter, with comments when needed before individual stories, and notes on sources and motifs in the back. A resource list includes books, Internet sites, and places to find Asian toys, crafts, and music to help set a mood for these tales.

One of the hardest challenges here was to write the various Asian languages in an understandable, pronounceable manner, without numerous and distracting diacritical marks. There was no perfect solution; I followed common usage for familiar words and wrote others in the most readable of transliterations, using marks only when essential *and* technically possible. You also will find the abbreviations C.E. (Common Era) and B.C.E. (Before the Common Era) to show dates—an acknowledgement that many Asian countries have their own calendars.

Since several orders are used for writing Asian names, it seemed least confusing to present first names followed by family names, except for certain historical figures. And I invite Muslim readers and friends to insert the proper blessing when I use the name of the Prophet Muhammad. Finally, the names of storytelling styles are in lower case except for those (like *Harikatha*, from the Lord Hari) which begin with proper nouns.

Introduction

To begin well is to be half done.
—Korean proverb

More than half of the earth's population lives in Asia today. Nine out of the world's fifteen largest cities are in Asia, and the Asian American population in the U.S. has doubled in the last decade. But too often the American view of Asia is best described by a favorite Japanese proverb, *One sees the sky through a hollow reed*. In this global age, the diverse nations of Asia have much to share with Americans. And what better way to learn than from the age-old yet contemporary art of the Asian storyteller? For Asia remains one of the world's richest sources of varied storytelling materials and techniques.

The stories in this anthology will help you glimpse a complex and changing region where village women draw well water as trains speed by; where high-tech factories overlook rice fields plowed by hand; and where some students write on slates while others program computers. Through stories, you can explore both the threads that connect Asian lands and the significant differences and conflicts found there.

At best, the tales, the tellers, and the techniques offered in this book can only hint at the larger story of Asia. For that started long, long ago as great kingdoms rose and fell across borders. In the early years, trade blossomed among Asian countries as well as with far-off lands. Religious beliefs and prejudices were exchanged in the region, along with silks, medicines, spices, and more. Fierce wars and battles alternated with peaceful times that nurtured rich cultural growth.

Then into Asia in recent centuries came European powers. Years of their colonial rule resulted in economic, cultural, and emotional damage in much of Asia. For they governed often with the sense of superiority shown by a British official in India who declared: "I have never found one scholar (of Oriental Studies) who could deny that a single shelf of a good European library was worth the whole native literature of India and Arabia."[1]

In this century Asia experienced a new round of war and regional conflict. Then, as many newly independent nations began to explore their own roots, Western influence again appeared: through Hollywood fantasies, multinationals, and American military bases. This new influence was not always welcome, as Indian journalist Claude Alvares points out:

> The import of Western institutions is now seen as attractive, inevitable, and necessary, even if we know that they are eventually alienating and degenerative. That we have attempted to ignore the immense reservoirs of human experience and talent which India has crafted over the centuries, is a major tragic story in itself.[2]

Fortunately, his words are part of a wake-up call raised by various Asian voices. Today a feeling is growing across the region that modernization need not mean Westernization; that the problems amidst the prosperity of the West—high divorce rates, violence, drugs, unwed mothers, lonely elders—may be too high a price to pay for material progress. Asian governments ranging from democratic to communist often agree on this point. As John Naisbitt explains, "the typical Western view of modernization, which encompasses ideas on civil liberty, freedom of speech and democracy, is strongly challenged by Asia. Asians place a high priority on family first and seek to devise a more communal and equitable form of development."[3]

In fact, the region's economic changes have begun to create partnerships among Asian powers, even former enemies. Neighbors look more often to each other for exchanges of knowledge and resources. This trend towards increased regional collaboration was expressed recently at the dedication of The Japan Foundation Asia Center, in words spoken by Maximo Kalaw, of Haribon Foundation, Philippines:

> We Asians need to accept our spiritual and ecological connections, and care for what is held in common in our region. The challenge is for us Asians—as diverse as we may be—to create together a just, equitable, peaceful, and sustainable world which will enrich all cultures.

It is indeed a wonderful time to take another look at Asia today through story, to learn both from Asian tellers and Asian American neighbors. It is a time for considering recent developments while reconsidering traditional values. Perhaps this welcome from KampungNet, a fine website by Singapore Muslims, best expresses the continuity amidst change which is Asia today:

> Selamat Datang! It means "Welcome!" in Malay ... KampungNet is inspired by the traditional Malay village, called a kampung. Although Malay kampungs have all but disappeared from the Singapore landscape as a result of rapid urbanisation, the spirit of caring and sharing, of community and togetherness, still remain strong among the Singapore Muslims who now make their homes in modern high-rise flats and apartments.[4]

Selamat Datang!

Storytellers and Styles 1

What is carved on rocks will wear away in time,
What is told from mouth to mouth will live forever.

—Vietnamese saying

Tracking down tales and finding tellers in Asia is not always easy; I have used everything from village gossip to e-mail in my journeys. The rhythm of the search sometimes echoes the rhythm of the culture; thus patience, flexibility, and a sense of humor are basic requirements. You cannot always find nicely printed notices or newsletters listing storytelling events, as this small true story demonstrates so well.

> One day, my story search took me to a small town in South India. There, someone told me that *if* I located the drummer who lived *somewhere* near the Kali temple, he *might* be able to help me find some storytelling.
>
> After a few wrong turns, I found myself at his home, drinking sweet tea with his friendly wife. Slowly I learned that yes, her husband was at a festival with storytelling. But no, she was not sure where. It was a village by a river and maybe it was near Palghat. So my husband and I trooped over to the local bus stand to find a ride to this perhaps place.
>
> Unfortunately, no one was certain which bus went closest to the village she'd described. At last, by a process of elimination, we were directed into one going in the right general direction. After the wheels were turning for a while, the driver shouted over his shoulder to everyone in the bus, asking for directions

to our destination. A babble of voices and instructions arose and an hour later we were left carefully on the edge of endless rice fields.

An arch, colorfully painted, stood framing a small footpath. I was excited, certain that its large Malayalam letters announced *Storytelling Festival*. We walked grandly under the arch and began slipping our way between rice fields, asking all we met where *katha* (story) was and following their kind but confusing hand gestures.

Finally we came to a river, crossed it, trudged up steep steps, and saw a sure sign of a storytelling gathering: a temporary tea stall. Since many stories can last up to eight hours, one needs tea and coffee to stay awake!

We settled in, drank tea, enjoyed a marvelous session of storytelling, then started back, only to find a flooded river. We ended up sleeping in the temple and, after some early morning tea and telling, we forded the river, slid through the rice fields, walked under the arch, and reached the road. As we waited for a bus to appear, another man joined us. He obviously spoke Malayalam and could thus read the sign on the arch. I opened my journal eagerly and asked him to translate the exact words on "that storytelling sign."

He read it slowly, then turned to me with a curious stare. He shrugged and said, "Madam, the sign says nothing about storytelling. It says only 'Vote Communist'!"

There are indeed many surprises on the road to Asian storytelling. But the rewards of the story search are well worth the sometimes endless bus rides or the dead ends one meets. Across the region, stories pass on history, preach peace, teach family planning, share values, and inspire change. They are shared by professionals, housewives, grandparents, librarians, teachers, beggars, and more. Come now to meet just a few of Asia's many tellers.

Nabe Shirasawa

"I heard so many tales when I was five, six, and seven. And I told them then, too," sighed eighty-six-year-old Nabe Shirasawa, one of the few remaining Ainu storytellers in Hokkaido, Japan. "My father once told me I would be important in preserving our Ainu culture. But I forgot what he said. I married and was so busy just trying to survive."

Survival was indeed a challenge for the Ainu people, once the original inhabitants but now a minority on Hokkaido Island. Japanese policies and prejudice in recent centuries resulted in loss of Ainu land, population, and language.

Fortunately, Nabe Shirasawa did not forget her stories, and to help a scholar's research some years ago, she told a traditional *yukara* (story) in a meeting with Ainu elders. "Everyone was thrilled to hear the real thing again," she said happily to us. Since then, she has been sharing the stories she can remember, even though some of the words are lost to her.

One afternoon in 1991, we sat together in her house near Sapporo. When she started to sing, her kind eyes looked at the floor. Her voice chanted soft words, and her hands sang a rhythm, the right fist tapping lightly against the left palm. We moved in storytime from her tiny home today to the older, prouder times of Ainu hunters free in their land.

"She is very special to us," said Ryukichi Ogawa, Ainu spokesman and my guide. "We try to preserve her energy so she can teach us. We have almost lost our stories. Our language was banned for years in this century and the few elders who remember the old tales are weak. Many are in nursing homes."

We finished our tea and then Nabe Shirasawa held my hand and rubbed my back, behind my heart, three times to the right. It was the traditional Ainu grandmother's greeting and farewell. It was a good way indeed to say goodbye.

Kamala Murthy

As we sat talking in her modest house in Thanjavur, India, Kamala Murthy showed the animation that makes her a popular storyteller. She is a teller in the sophisticated and demanding *Harikatha* style of India. For this style, she told me, one must know thousands of religious verses along with classical and folk styles of Indian music, and several Indian languages. One must remember the Hindu epics like *Ramayana* and *Mahabharata* as well as stories of the many saints, and hundreds of little anecdotes and tales to insert as needed into longer stories.

"I have four sons and two daughters so it is very difficult for me to manage my home and keep up with my storytelling," she said in a familiar complaint. But she did—and does—manage as one of the very few female *bhagavatars* (tellers) to perform in temples, auditoriums, and for marriage ceremonies. Her storytelling can be hours long and distant, even in Malaysia and Sri Lanka. But it must also be very short when she shares tales over All India Radio. Those stories can only be ten to twenty minutes, a challenge for a style where all-night tellings were frequent in earlier years.

Kamala Murthy started telling at the age of eight, working with her *guru* for several hours every day, and following him to his storytellings. Her father was a constant help and encouragement as well. After her marriage at sixteen, she stopped telling Harikatha for three years but, urged by her husband, began again. She loves Harikatha and feels strongly about recent changes in the artform: "Some of today's bhagavatars want only to have people laugh and enjoy. They have forgotten the true purpose of Harikatha—to offer devotion to God and to instruct people on the important side of life, the spiritual."

Sachiko Yokoyama

In the Tohoku region, story heartland of northern Japan, in an old home complete with dark beams and an *irori* (firepit), a storytelling class goes on. Once a year, over fifty men and women gather here for a six-week storytelling course led by Sachiko Yokoyama. She tells tales one minute in a loud, comic style, the next in a quiet style, her voice taking the huskiness of an old Japanese grandmother. Along with the tales come her comments and then the students share as well.

Sachiko Yokoyama is a traditional yet innovative teller who travels widely in Japan, sharing tales in schools, community centers, libraries, museums, and festivals. Sachiko came late to storytelling and seems to make up for lost time—so great is her energy and enthusiasm. Although she heard many stories growing up, she was pulled into fulltime telling only when her youngest son died in an accident at the age of twenty.

"I realized then that I never had enough time for him, to tell him stories," she told me. "I was so busy trying to work with my husband at his printing press. Too busy trying to make a good living. So after my son died, I made a vow to his spirit. I promised to tell the stories to others that I should have told him." Even today, over a decade later, she always offers part of what she receives as a storytelling gift to her son's photograph proudly resting on the family altar.

Yokoyamasan also spends much time seriously encouraging Japanese youngsters to tell. She regularly helps a high school group of tellers and also guides elementary-age tellers in an after-school program. Some of these youngsters share stories in the *Long Ago House*, an old farmhouse and museum in her hometown. Fourteen-year-old Yoko, one of her students and proud teller of thirty tales, shares what she has learned: "Choose a story that you like, and not because of tradition or what others think!"

Young Sook Song

"I think that Korean children today need to hear many stories, new and old. So many children live now in high towers of apartments in Seoul. Their own past seems far from them. Stories must give them their heritage. And stories from other countries, like Japan, can help world peace."

These words were spoken with quiet conviction by Young Sook, a storyteller able to bridge the gulf of bitter war memories separating Korea from neighboring Japan. Her husband's work in a bank has taken them to the U.S., Japan, and Korea. While in Japan, she studied storytelling at Tokyo Children's Library and became interested in *kamishibai* storytelling cards.

Since Young Sook is one of Korea's early library science graduates, she returned from Japan eager to promote storytelling for Korean children. She started a small library for children and began storytelling circles of college students and adults. Young Sook now teaches storytelling to all ages in college classes, community centers, and reading schools. She would like to see more storytelling in Korean libraries and schools, along with more recognition for Korean writers: "From the West we get too many stories from Disney recently. We have wonderful Korean folk tales, plus a growing modern children's literature, with talented writers and illustrators who should be shared through storytelling and reading."

Putha Touch

Putha Touch longs to tell tales again in Cambodia, but he may never have the chance. Putha grew up hearing stories often in his home and weekly in school there. Later, as a teacher in Cambodia, he regularly used folk tales and remembers which were told to different grades. His great interest in storytelling led him to gather stories, even in the midst of a terrible war, from elders weakened but eager to pass them on.

Putha came to Seattle as a refugee because there was no other choice, and the move left him vulnerable. "In Cambodia, I felt strong and capable. Here I seem so little and Americans so big and powerful." Sharing stories from his lovely homeland was one way for him to rediscover self-respect and confidence. We spent many long afternoons in his apartment, traveling on the sound of his mother's gentle chants and the smell of her incense back to a Cambodia strong and proud, one which could boast of the great King Jayavarman VII, the magnificent Angkor Wat, and the wily national folk hero, Judge Rabbit.

Putha's true stories described the pain of many modern Cambodians; once he told of returning to his home during a truce:

> I came to Phnom Penh and saw the proud international bank kneeling on the ground and, next to it, a favorite temple, now a garbage heap. I stopped by my former high school: trees and grass like a jungle surrounded it. I started down a road with no sign, feeling close to my house. Suddenly, a bony hand touched my shoulder. I turned and saw an old lady. I recognized my mother's friend although her face had changed. It held such a great grief. Yes, her whole family had been killed except her. I could not barricade my tears as she

> pointed to the empty space with broken bits of walls—that was my home. And not only my house was gone, but my brothers and relatives had disappeared too. The pool where I always swam every evening was a dirty pond. Neighbors used to gather to chat, tell folk tales, and play at night there. Now only death, glass pieces, and sad stories remained.

Wang Yulan, introduced by Kate Stevens

Wang Yulan was born in a small village in the southern reaches of the Yi Meng Mountain Range in Shandong Province. She was the child of a poor peasant farmer, one child among many, coming somewhere in the neglected middle. Stories her father told, songs her mother sang were her only schooling and she went early to work in the fields. She sought out stories at work breaks, at a neighbor's, wherever she could. And if the men teased her for tagging along, she gave as good as she got, and kept on listening.

Marriage at seventeen was a shock, for her father-in-law had been a yamen clerk in his day and kept the new bride very properly close to the family compound. In her isolation it was stories remembered that consoled her and, rebellious always, whenever she could she shared them with the other new brides as well.

Before many years passed her husband died, and then her parents-in-law one after the other. Since she had no sons of her own, an elder brother gave her his youngest boy. To keep the child alive in a time of drought, flood, and civil war, she wandered from village to village, begging as she went.

Now the stories she loved quite literally saved her life. Because she could tell and tell well, when she begged, people gave. Eventually she was able to return to her home village where as life became easier, her son could support her. In 1986, *Tales by Four Elders,* which included twenty-three of her tales, was published to great acclaim and since then she has lived in honored leisure as her village's "Basket Full of Stories."[1]

V. Sambasivam

"We are doing an operation to purify the minds of the audience," explained V. Sambasivam, a teller whose repertoire includes *Anna Karenina* along with modern stories from his native state of Kerala. His popular style of telling, *kathaprasangam*, is unique to this lovely South Indian state, which has nearly 100 percent literacy, a low birth rate, and, at times, a communist government. Kathaprasangam started in the twentieth century to popularize regional literature and to challenge societal problems of caste, corruption, and inequality.

V. Sambasivan tells his own original stories and novels as well, all in a very theatrical style, backed up by five musicians who play a creative combination of Western and Indian instruments. He started telling in 1949 to support his college studies, then worked as a teacher at Sanskrit High School. In 1975, during the censorship of the Emergency period declared by Indira Gandhi, he was arrested for telling a story by a leftist Bengali writer. Forced to leave his job, he then turned to telling fulltime. His audiences can be in the thousands and he tells both in villages and cities. During the busy season, December to May, he often has two programs a night. When he's not performing, he teaches others through a local Progressive Storytellers' Association, studies, rests, and stays in touch with his five children.

Kyoko Matsuoka

Kyoko Matsuoka has been an inspiration to countless Japanese tellers for many years. It all began when she opened a *bunko*, a small home library, in 1967. In 1974, along with three other bunkos, it became Tokyo Children's Library, which now has twenty thousand volumes of books and research materials. The library is a great resource for storytellers: its two-year courses in telling have been completed by over one thousand people to date, and among its many publications on storytelling is a very popular series of booklets, *Ohanashi no Rosoku* (Story Candle), which has sold over one million copies.

While directing the library and guiding numerous storytellers, Matsuokasan has also written and translated 124 books, many of them used eagerly by Japanese tellers. She wishes to offer the best stories from many cultures, to address the need she sees today in Japanese listeners for "some inner psychological mechanism, some feeling of self-dignity, a glimpse of journey into self, a quality of fantasy and 'beyond this world' elements not found in traditional Japanese folk tales, where spirits and human often mingle more on this earth."

She is pleased to see storytelling growing in schools, and to see the growth and change in Japanese storytelling itself. "Many Japanese tellers still don't recognize the power of storytelling to ask questions, to address social issues," she told me. "And they don't share enough true stories yet. But it will come soon. Japanese storytelling has a long history. Today, tellers from different styles are starting to interact, old lines are being crossed, storytelling is entering new areas. Japanese storytelling is very much in a state of flux now. The years to come will surely bring exciting change. Wait and see."

No one can predict the future of Asian storytelling, but a final image from the countryside of Japan offers reassurance:

> In the mountain's shadow, the old farmhouse seemed to float on rice fields. Inside, Takeyo Ito, dressed in traditional farmer's cloth and wearing her eighty-four years proudly, began to tell. She told in a quiet voice, her hands content with small gestures, her face sliding often into smiles. Her words flowed out as her grandsons urged her on with frequent responses—"Hah" "ah ra ra." Hours and stories flew by. Then a girl of fourteen, in stylish shorts, walked in and sat shyly next to her great-grandmother. Above the two was a scroll advising in careful characters, *Have big ears to hear and a small mouth to speak little as you listen with kind eyes.*
>
> The girl started a tale and as the words came out, the eyes in her great grandmother's face looked down. Her head nodded gently as her lips moved silently, following the girl's words. It was a duet of spirit, through story. And in that shared moment, in that shared telling, story triumphed over time and flowed from the past through this child proudly into tomorrow.

Storytelling Tools

2

The mouth tastes food,
The heart tastes words.
—Hmong proverb

Asian storytellers use familiar storytelling tools: the voice, words, gestures, music, props, and more. But the Asian teller, whether trained long years in a particular style, sharing a memorized text, or simply telling as her grandmother did, shapes the tools in different ways.

LANGUAGE

Images

Words paint pictures, and certain words share images understood at once by Asian listeners. In Buddhist and Hindu cultures, the lotus is a sign of purity, and the white elephant is royal indeed. Across Asia, the bamboo is a symbol of beauty and gentle strength while the coconut tree is thought both graceful and giving, since every part of it is useful.

Sometimes such a single word or image is enough; sometimes longer comparisons or formulas are used. Here is a sampling gathered from traditional Asian telling.

Korean

- as lonely as a single wild goose
- as light as the wing of a dragonfly
- as modest as a ripe grain of rice (hanging its head)
- as soft as bean curd
- as wrinkled as a dried pumpkin

Indian

- as sweet as jasmine
- skin like sandalwood
- strutting like a peacock
- trembling like a water lily
- stinging like a scorpion's bite

Pathan of Pakistan

- eyebrows arched like hunting bows
- large eyes gleaming like bullets
- only sorrow remaining as food for parents (after the death of a son)

Cambodian

- A king's reign is like a flawless crown made from a garland of jasmine flowers.
- His order is an ax from heaven.
- His glory is like a roar in all directions.

Hmong

- as pretty as a dragon's daughter
- Sun is Grandmother bringing the red blanket.
- Sky is nailed up with 3000 silver nails and 3600 golden nails.
- Thunder is like a rooster with a knife of fire, which is lightning.

Riddles

Many an Asian tale has a riddle sequence—a scene where riddles are used in courting, in settling an argument without weapons, or in answering a challenge. At times a riddle is answered by another riddle, no matter how impossible. Since riddles also paint pictures, here are a few images to try:

Japanese

- a white horse with no bones *(tofu)*
- white hair when young, turning black when old *(writing brush)*
- a one-eyed goblin with one leg *(sewing needle)*

Indian

- A mother carries her children around her neck. *(coconut tree)*
- A man makes money by burning what he makes. *(potter)*
- A ghost speaks from a dry piece of wood. *(gun)*
- A flower shuts by day and opens at night. *(mat)*

Filipino

- two boats with only one pilot *(shoes)*
- planted in the afternoon, harvested at dawn *(stars)*
- When the vines are pulled, the birds sing. *(church bells)*
- A dangerous telegram, for death often results. *(gun)*

Vietnamese

- Born in a bamboo thicket, I close up in winter, to open when summer returns. *(fan)*
- Five boys hold two long bamboo poles and push white buffaloes into a cave. *(fingers, chopsticks, rice)*

Burmese

- a cup of milk spilled over the whole countryside *(the moon)*
- looks like a bird, and can fly, yet has no life. *(airplane)*

Repetitions and Lists

In Asian ballads and epics, listing words or images is a time-honored technique. And saying the list at very high speed, tongue twisterlike, is a sign of sure talent. During "The Song of Silk" from *p'ansori* (Korean operatic storytelling), forty-five types of silks and ninety-seven pieces of furniture are quickly named as they emerge from a gourd. And "The Song of Food," later in the same tale (*Heungbu Nolbu*), lists fifty-two different foods when they spill out.[1]

Repetition, of parts of a line or of similar images, is another common effect used by various storytellers. Here is a small sample from "At Break of Day," in Beijing Drumsinging, another richly musical storytelling style:

A cartwheel of a moon sinks to the west—
you can't hear, from the drum watchtower,
you can't hear the watch-block struck,
you can't hear the little bell shook,
you can't hear the long bell being rapped,
you can't hear the big bell hit,
For the watchman in charge sleeps thundrously.[2]

In the same story, the last word is repeated to begin the next line in a chainlike manner very popular in East Asian poetry and word play:

Hills growing dark clouds,
clouds covering green pines,
pines hiding the old temple,
the temple sheltering a hillside monk,
the hillside monk in Buddha's hall strikes the wooden fish.[3]

Word Sounds and Play

As the Asian teller tells a tale, her words may evoke group memories and regional feelings. In Asia are found hundreds of languages. India, the Philippines, Indonesia, and China have especially large numbers. Yet even countries sharing one predominant language, like Korea or Japan, have many dialects. Each language and dialect carries a sense of homeland, for identity is bound up in the sounds of words, the rhythms spoken, the accents used.

A young mother in northern Japan told me that "folktales in my own dialect give a feeling of belonging to my children, while the memories of the old sounds make the grandparents happy." She worried that regional identities were threatened by the increasing use of standard Japanese over national media. Her fears are echoed in other Asian countries. In Thailand, Dr. Wajuppa Tossa uses storytelling to promote pride in the Lao language of her homeland, Isan (Northeastern Thailand), especially among those who now prefer speaking Bangkok Thai to appear sophisticated.

Each language has its own rhymes, and many Asian tellers use rhyme cleverly both within and between lines. Puns are also widely found and enjoyed, especially in languages like Chinese or Vietnamese where different tones produce very different meanings.

A rich range of onomatopoeia also delights story listeners in various Asian languages. Japanese probably has the best variety of sound words. Here are just a few to try:

chira chira	(chee - rah)	a weak light flickering
choko choko	(choe - koe)	to toddle
doshin	(doe - shin)	something heavy falling
doki doki	(doe - kee)	a frightened heartbeat
gacha gacha	(gah - chah)	to rattle, clatter
naku naku	(nah - koo)	to cry tears
niko niko	(nee - koe)	to smile warmly
pacha pacha	(pah - chah)	a light splash
soro soro	(soe - roe)	to walk slowly

Openings and Closings

"Many years ago, a big wind came and blew me to a great wood where I saw this happen ..." So would a Hmong grandmother begin a tale in her own language. A Pathan teller from Pakistan might use flowery words which meant: "Hear the wonderful rose-colored story with which I'll remove the rust from your aching heart." In Japan, *Mukashi, mukashi* (mu-ka-shee, mu-ka-shee) is the classic "long, long ago."

Both openings and closings in some epic or ballad styles of telling might be prayers or rituals to praise and thank a god or a spirit, at times with an offering. Closings in folk traditions may be quite straight forward, as in the Japanese *Oshimai* (O-shee-my)—Finished. Or they can be more involved, like this especially long one from Orissa, India:

My story ended.
The flower plant died.
Well, flower plant, why did you die?
The black cow ate me up.

Well, black cow, why did you eat away the plant?
The herdsman did not watch me.
Well, herdsman, why did you not watch the cow?
The eldest daughter did not give me food.
Well, eldest daughter, why did you not give him food?
The child wept.
Well, child, why did you weep?
I was bitten by a dusty black ant.
Well, black ant, why did you bite the child?
I live under the earth and when I find soft flesh,
bite it I must.[4]

GESTURE

A Range of Movement

The use of gesture in, and within, different Asian cultures shows a whole range of restraint. Japanese librarians favor a very quiet telling style, often lighting a candle and telling with hands folded, face subdued. Professional Japanese tellers from the sophisticated *rakugo* style also do not use total body movement—they kneel and move from that position. Yet their facial and vocal expressions are extremely helpful to audiences: the different body postures, voices, and shifts of focus clearly show varied emotions and characters.

Indian tellers in many professional styles often stand and move with their whole body actively miming or gesturing. Hands are eloquent and ever-moving; eyes offer inner glimpses of a tale. I once watched an eighty-year-old master of *Chakyar kuttu*, a South Indian form of telling where improvisation and facial expression play a large role. Using only his eyes, with eye muscles I never knew existed, he showed the flight of a moth to and from a flame.

To achieve such control, students in this style practice moving eyebrows up and down at different paces. Then they hold their eyes wide open with fingers, and move the eyes slowly:

- up and down
- in big circles
- in slow figure eights
- diagonally top to bottom and back

In *ottan thullal*, another South Indian style, hands are used with great elegance and power. Storytelling students increase their strength by these exercises:

- Hold hands out in front. Make fists, then move them up and down. Next, move fists around in circles, to the left, then to the right.
- Hold hands out in front, fingers spread apart. Keeping arms straight, twist hands right-left-right-left. Increase speed slowly but definitely.
- Make circle of right thumb and first finger, same with left. Hold other fingers spread out and straight, in front of chest, with elbows down and relaxed. Holding circles steady, flutter remaining three fingers on each hand up and down, at increasing speeds.

In Korean p'ansori, the teller usually stands and gestures with one hand holding a fan, sometimes adding a fall to the ground for dramatic effect, while some Chinese tellers use a formal set of gestures, many adapted from Beijing Opera. Storyteller and teacher Putha Touch recalled hearing stories in lectures from Cambodian monks with quiet gestures, and from older people relaxing in the sun and moving little.

Gesture and Meaning

Since we also share culture through gesture, anyone telling a tale must be sensitive to the meaning of gestures used. Some meanings are easily observed, like pointing to the nose, not the chest, to mean "I/my" in China and Japan. Some are more subtle and taught best from someone of that culture, even if it takes a while. Once I told a version of *Kasa Jizo* for some Japanese librarians. Two years later, I stayed with one, now my good friend, Makisan, and she said, "May I mention one thing about your *Kasa Jizo* we would like you to change? When you had the man sell hats, you shouted and used your hands in a big way. That is Osaka style. But your story came from cold, snowy Tohoku. There, the man would sell quietly, his voice calm. No loud gestures, no shouts. Please remember and give the true flavor of that story."

Emotion is shared in different ways across Asia. And traditional values often are reflected in gestures, such as those of Burmese leader Aung San Suu Kyi, here described by a friend:

> [She], in my view, is an examplar of what we Burmese regard as seemly.... To take a small example: the courtesy and deference shown to those older than oneself even by a few years [she indicates by] a slight inclination of the body when passing before them, an economy and refinement of gesture, a tone of voice and a choice of language implying respect.[5]

Certain gestures may possibly be offensive or confusing. These also vary from culture to culture, but here are a few which could be avoided in telling Asian tales:

- Beckoning towards you, with the palm up to mean "Come," for that is used with animals.
- Touching the head, since that is disrespectful to this sacred part of a person.
- Prolonging eye contact with elders, which might not show enough respect.
- Touching or pointing towards something with your feet, which is insulting because feet are the lowest part of the body.
- Pointing your finger directly at someone, since that could be taken as a scolding or insult.

Music and Sound

Music is an integral part of many Asian telling techniques; some stories are chanted or told entirely in song. Tellers may accompany themselves or be accompanied by musicians playing varied instruments, often mixing song and speech in most effective ways.

Voice and Other Instruments

The voice can be finely trained and expressive, as described in "The Song of Kwangdae," a poem about p'ansori:

> *The lifting voice is like a lofty peak soaring,*
> *The rolling down voice like the sound of a water-fall ...*
> *A clear floating voice like the whooping of a crane in blue sky,*
> *A sudden bouncing voice seems to be a peal of thunder,*
> *A rapid changing voice is like a desolate cold wind among the bare trees.*[6]

Kate Stevens, who has studied Chinese storytelling styles, describes the music of the vibrant Beijing Drumsong from her first enchantment with it in Taipei:

> Two musicians took their seats at the table, with a three-string Chinese banjo and a four-string spike fiddle. The singer entered, took up her clapper and drumstick, and gave a commanding glance at the two musicians, who followed her lead as she began a rousing drum pattern. A pause for some spoken words of introduction, another instrumental interlude and then the singing began.
>
> It was singing such as I had never heard before, akin to speech. Her voice rose, then tumbled down from one shimmering note to another, supported by the strings. Suddenly the rhythm quickened, the melody simplified, the clapper beat became continuous. Then all too soon, with one final slow triumphant couplet, it was over. But I wanted more.[7]

Bells, drums, a long-necked lute, a one-stringed fiddle, wooden clappers, a clay pot, a wooden block—all enhance different Asian storytelling styles. One of the most interesting instruments is the bow used in the *villu pattu* style of South India. It is a large bow with bells strung on it, and as the teller tells a ballad, he hits the bow to make rhythms and to underline story parts. He is accompanied by several others who sing, play instruments, and respond to his telling.

Rhythm, Melody, and Meaning

Melody is rich and varied in Asian telling, but stepping outside of one's own culture through music is very challenging. Melodies and rhythms speak most clearly to those who understand them, as I learned in Bangladesh.

During a storytelling collaboration with two fine musicians there, whenever I felt the need for music that went faster or with more passion to underline a dramatic part of the story, they would use a *raga* (melodic line) which sounded far too mild and quiet to my ears. When I gently questioned them, they replied, "Our audience feels the mood through the notes of the raga. They know immediately all that that raga portrays, whether it is a feeling of pathos, of great joy, or of loss. The raga speaks to them far more clearly than extra noise, a faster rhythm, or a show of outer emotion."

The notes to two ragas used in Harikatha telling are written here to give you a taste of their mood. But remember, as Indian musician Annie Penta warns, that "one cannot really write down the notes for a melody in a raga and have someone play it on a piano with a Western-trained idea of pitch. The way of moving from note to note, the strength and duration of the note, the exact tuning are so very important."

SĀRANG — Early afternoon. Uses both the 7ths; no 3rd or 6th (pentatonic). Principal mood: heroic

BHIMPALĀSI — Uses flattened 3rd and 7th. Principal mood: sad but dignified.

The rhythms used in many storytelling styles add greatly to the mood and tension of the story; musicians work closely with tellers to enrich the tale. In Indian ottan thullal, nine different rhythmic cycles are used, while in Southeast Asian ballads, beat cycles of 2, 4, and 8 are common. In his splendid book on p'ansori, Marshall Pihl[8] lists the five primary rhythmic cycles and moods, from slowest to fastest:

chinyang cho	meter: 18/8	accents: 1,5,6	poignant
chung mori	12/4	1,9	composed
chung chung mori	12/8	1,9	elegant
chajin mori	12/8	1	lively
hwi mori	4/4	1	urgent

Improvisation

In certain Asian styles, improvisation, at times enriched by collaboration, is important. Some less formal styles offer opportunities for tellers to improvise in ways funded by local governments: creatively inserting modern messages of family planning and rural development, or about political candidates. Other styles are rich in the use of side stories and clever comments.

In *burra katha* of India, a main teller keeps the story going while a helper injects current events and asks questions, thus making an old tale relevant to modern listeners. They might, for example, compare Sita's lovely marriage in the *Ramayana* epic to the ostentatious, wasteful marriages recently put on by several Indian movie stars, politicians, and businesspeople.

In the sophisticated *Chakyar kuttu* of Kerala, the *Chakyar* (teller) tells alone, using skillful improvisation and weaving new images into verses from the past. In this style traditionally, the teller could also insult people without fear of punishment. Joseph Kunnath, a friend and story collector, described "a Chakyar who wished to remind the king that his ministers were not very bright. Thus he told of Hanuman, the great monkey, jumping from rock to rock to rock. He said, 'Hanuman jumped from empty spot to empty spot to empty spot,' while pointing to each of the ministers' heads, one after another after another."

Props

Asia offers a wider variety of storytelling props than any other world region. Here are just a few, to suggest ideas for your telling, writing, illustration, and for further research.

Costume

Clothes communicate much— from the horsehair hat and scholarly clothes of a male p'ansori singer to the colorful costume of a wandering Indian singer portraying Lord Siva in both story and appearance. In Bangladesh, I once watched a famous teller transform a long scarf into a sari, a turban, a well rope, reins, a road, a whip, a bundle, food, and a baby during one long tale!

Patas

Patas are vertical scrolls, up to twenty feet long, with some ten to fifteen rectangular panels showing scenes from a story. The stories themselves vary from older tales of gods to newer court cases of accidents and crimes, tales of the Indian freedom fight, or stories about the dowry system, family planning, or widow remarriage.

The scrolls are unrolled as the story is told by either Hindu or Muslim tellers of Northeast India. Performers must wander in search of work, often going to houses where someone has died and telling to honor the deceased. Today, since this storytelling style provides little pay or security, young men are attracted instead to factory jobs and citylife, and so, unfortunately, the form may slowly disappear.

Phad

The *phad* is a long storytelling scroll (from nine to twenty-five feet) found in Rajasthan state, North India. It is used by a teller who travels from village to village. The scroll is set up on bamboo poles, usually outdoors; and as the *bhopa* (teller) tells, he sings, dances, and plays a many-stringed fiddle. His wife accompanies him with song and illuminates the relevant story scenes with a lantern. Members of the audience join in on familiar refrains and follow the story eagerly, often all night. The most commonly told story is that of Pabuji, a fourteenth-century regional hero.

Kavad

The *kavad*, an amazing storytelling box, also is found in North India. It contains many panels, each illustrated with scenes from a story, usually about Lord Rama. The teller tells the tale as he unfolds the panels, first on one side, then the other. After each set of side panels is fully opened, two smaller doors remain in the center. At last they are opened and the story ends with an image of a main character or deity.

Tankas

Related to the painted scrolls used in Korean and Japanese temples, these ornate silk hangings from Tibet often illustrated Buddhist themes, including hell's tortures and the lives of saints. The wandering Tibetan tellers of the great epic *Gesar* were said to have used such tankas, with their intricate illustrations of the story. At the Tibetan School of Drama now in North India, I heard of a teller in Lhasa, Tibet, who not only used the tanka but also took tiny characters from the story out of his pocket and let them run up and over his nose! Truly a magical storyteller ...

Hmong Story Cloths

These exquisite story cloths, portraying legends or daily life, show how a new visual narrative form can evolve. The Hmong people, who fled from Laos to seek safety in Thai refugee camps, combined their stories, their sewing skill, and their economic needs into the creation of story cloths. Hmong refugees who moved to the U.S. brought this new form, inspired by their traditional stitched *paj ntaub* (flower cloth). The cloths provide income today, but also recall a homeland and its stories to many, as Blia Xiong explains:

> I did this piece because I think that after all the older people, the generations, after they're all gone, it will really help the younger people to know. What we're doing here and why. How we got here. Because if nobody tells them, they'll never know.[9]

Kamishibai

The kamishibai teller earlier in this century cycled from place to place in Japan, carrying large, hand-painted story cards. Each twelve- to sixteen-card set visually related, in sequence, either an entire tale or part of one (popular serials stretched on for months). The teller gathered a crowd, sold candy and rice snacks to the audience, then told kamishibai tales—samurai stories, Chinese legends, science fiction, funny tales, even the "Lone Ranger." Today, both lovely handmade sets and printed cards are used in libraries and schools, since the traveling tellers are very rare.

Fan

A folding fan is a part of both Japanese rakugo and Korean p'ansori telling. In p'ansori it is used mainly for emphasis and dramatic effect. In rakugo, it can portray various items: a sword, a *shamisen* (lute), a pipe, a pole to carry things, a pot, a writing brush, a bowl, and a screen. To show the passing seasons, the *hanashika* (teller) might raise and lower the fully opened fan in front of his face four times while giving the fruit-seller's seasonal cries.

SETTING AND AUDIENCE

Stories are told in various settings and times today in Asia. They are shared at bedtime or mealtime, at harvest, at fairs and festivals, in libraries and schools, on busy market streets, in places of worship.

In many settings, audience members repeat a refrain to assure the teller that they are listening, or offer other types of feedback. During an ottan thullal performance in South India, pleased listeners can go right up to the stage to offer some cash. In an older, classical style of Japanese telling, *kodan*, the regular listeners might call out to less talented tellers, "Couldn't you recite something that won't disturb us from sleeping?"

Some Asian settings are very active. Outside the compound of a Kerala temple, I heard a teller address noisy listeners while chants blared from the loudspeaker, temple bells and drums sounded nearby, and temple elephants circled by every five minutes, along with a large, loud crowd.

Kate Stevens shares a lively teahouse storytelling setting in older Beijing, as described by her teacher:

> The audience came to enjoy their favorite performers, shouting out "hao!" (bravo) at appropriate points. Hot towels flew through the air to waiting patrons, tea water arced from great pots into glasses. Children ran up and down the aisles, grown-ups cracked melon seeds and chatted. The audience was there to be part of a lively social occasion wherein Chinese culture and history were celebrated in story. So familiar were the tales that any misstep, any subtle variation of music or text drew instant attention.[10]

At times the setting for Asian storytelling is theatrical, at other times daily and ordinary, and sometimes very festive. In many Indian celebrations, palm leaf, bamboo, bright paper, and flowers are turned into eyecatching decorations—an exciting backdrop for long stories. Drawings may also be made on the ground with vivid colors or arranged from flowers. In some temples, exquisite brass oil lamps glow beyond the present, pulling the listener into the power of story.

Yet whether the tale is told in a bright Osaka community center or on a moonlit night in a Southeast Asian village, the audience listens and listens well. Turn the page to find the tales they hear.

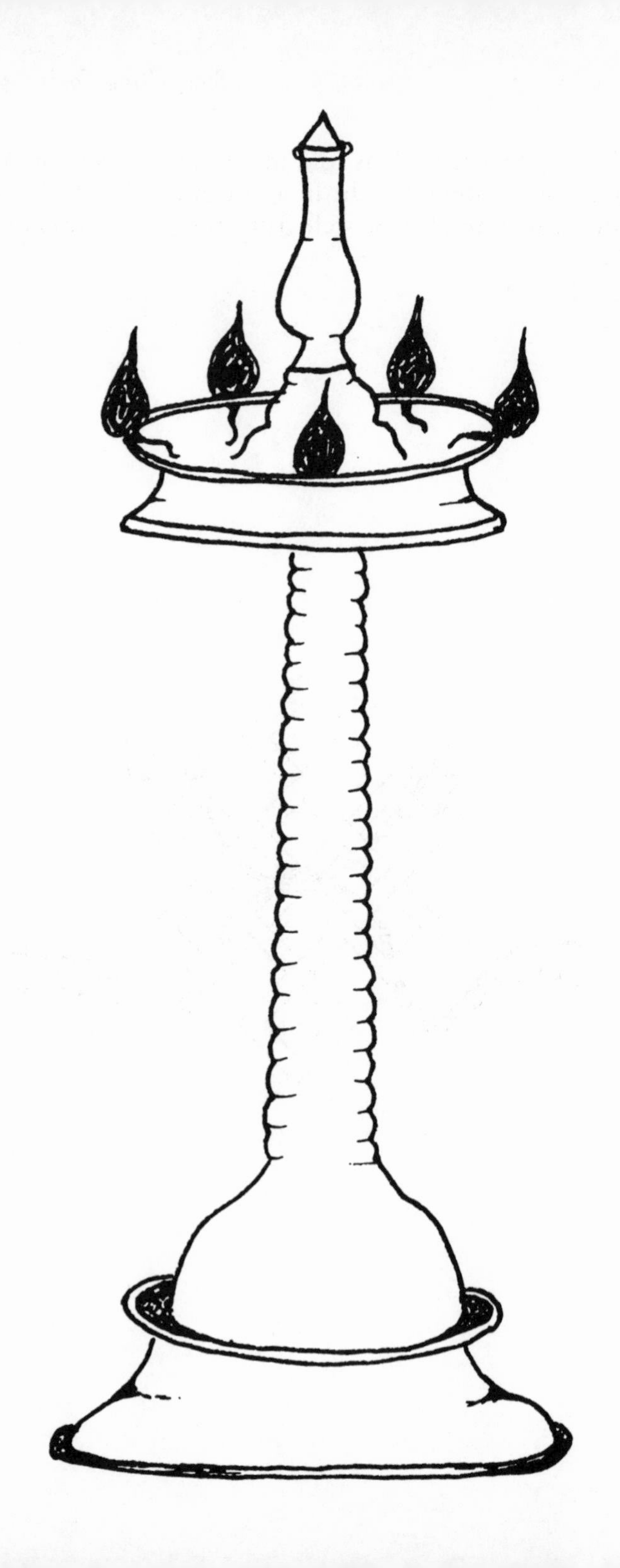

3 Harmony and Friendship

As a bamboo tube makes a round jet of water,
So taking counsel together molds men to one mind.

—Malay proverb

A theme of harmony runs through much of Asian society. The Korean flag includes the round yin-yang image as a symbol of balance. In China, the lengths of bamboo pipes cut to give the first musical pitches were calculated to make music in harmony with the universe.

Putting the needs of the group over those of the individual is taught from birth in many Asian societies, to encourage cooperation. Vertical societies once were common features in the region, supporting harmony by a strict class hierarchy from Confucian thought (in parts of East Asia) or from the caste system (in parts of South Asia).

Friendship in Asian countries is strong and longlasting, nurtured by values of loyalty and obligation. Friends often can see each other on a regular basis—there is limited mobility in some Asian cultures, and people have a relaxed sense of time in many settings. Childhood and school friends frequently remain close for decades: spending time together at the well in quiet villages, playing the latest video games in sprawling cities, or enjoying school trips when young, then sharing opportunities and celebrations later in life.

Two Friends

HMONG PEOPLE OF LAOS

Two friends were in the forest when suddenly they heard a horse bear coming. Frightened and thinking only of himself, the elder boy climbed quickly up the closest tree. The other boy, who couldn't climb well, threw himself down on the ground, pretending to be dead. The bear came up and circled round the body. He put his head close to the boy's face for a long time, then at last he left.

After many minutes of quiet, the boy in the tree came down, ran to his friend, and asked, "What was the bear doing? He stayed near you for so long."

His friend replied, "He was talking to me. He gave me some good advice. He said, 'Don't trust a friend that doesn't help you in time of danger.'"

Yamanba of the Mountain

JAPAN

The help of elders supports harmony in society, and friends can come in many forms, as this tale suggests. A yamanba, *found in Japanese folklore, usually lives on mountains, is quite fierce, and can change shapes.*

Mukashi, mukashi ... Long ago in a quiet Japanese village, people feared the yamanba who lived at the top of a nearby mountain.

When rains fell too hard on their crops, people said, "It's her fault, that yamanba. She likes to make trouble."

When snows piled up high on their houses, people said, "It's her fault, that yamanba. She loves to make trouble."

When great winds whipped through the village, people said, "It's her fault, that yamanba. She always makes trouble."

However, no one had ever seen the yamanba. No one had ever heard the yamanba. They didn't even know if she was real. They only passed on the terrible tales that their parents had heard from their parents.

Now, one fall day, a fierce wind suddenly blew, *byuu, byuu.* Rain poured down, *za, za, za, za.* Hailstones fell too, *ba-ra, ba-ra.* Then a terrifying voice roared, "I am the yamanba's new baby. We both want rice balls right now. If you don't bring *mochi* to us soon, we'll eat you all up!"

Everyone trembled. Everyone cried. Everyone spoke at once.

"I was so scared."

"Who was that?"

"He said they'll eat us."

"Hurry, let's make rice balls right now."

Quickly they boiled the rice, *gu-tsu, gu-tsu.* In a hurry, they pounded it, *den-da-go, den-da-go.* Without stopping, they shaped the rice into fine mochi. When all the rice balls were finished, someone asked, "Now who will deliver them?"

No one spoke. Even the bravest men and women were silent. Everyone had helped to make the mochi, but no one wanted to face that frightful yamanba. Finally, a small woman stepped up. "I'm the oldest here," she said. "I've lived a good life, and I'm ready to die if I must. I will go and try."

Voices suddenly wrapped round her, thanking her again and again. Two young men who knew the mountain were chosen to guide her, and they all set off the next day. Higher and higher and higher they climbed. Soon, the wind howled and pushed against them.

"We can't take anymore," cried the two men as the wind bounced them around.

"Have courage!" the old woman shouted, clinging to a pine tree. But when the wind finally died down, the old woman couldn't find the men. They had run away.

"What young cowards," she sighed. "Well, I guess I'll go on alone."

Up and up she climbed until she reached the mountaintop. In the clearing there, no wind was heard. Yet it was not at all quiet.

"*Wan! Wan!*" The bellows of a huge baby punched the air. Slowly and a little fearfully, the woman crept toward the sounds. They grew louder and louder until, suddenly, a door jumped open and a huge yamanba rushed out. She charged right into the old woman, knocking her flat on the ground. The poor woman looked up to see a fierce face with a hungry mouth and enormous teeth. She closed her eyes, waiting for death.

"*Araa*, what have I done?" cried the yamanba. "*Sumimasen.* I am so sorry. I didn't see you. Are you hurt?"

With many apologies, she carefully helped the woman up.

"I was just going for water. Please come inside and I'll make us some nice tea," offered the yamanba.

Much surprised, the woman followed her, and soon the two were sharing lovely green tea around a warm fire.

"I have brought your mochi," whispered the old woman at last.

"Wonderful," beamed the yamanba. "How very kind of

you. After my son was born yesterday, I was so hungry for mochi. Since he could fly at birth, I sent him down to ask nicely for some. I hope he was polite and didn't cause any trouble?"

Afraid to answer, the woman simply took out the mochi. Later, after the three had a fine meal, she said, "That was delicious. Thank you. But now, I really must return."

Looking ready to cry, the yamanba pleaded, "No, please don't go. I get lonely up here. And I'm so busy with the new baby. Couldn't you stay and help me for a little while?"

Now, the old woman did not really want to stay near such a fierce-looking yamanba, one she had heard so much about. Yet though she still did not trust her, she also was afraid to refuse.

So, day after day, the old woman worked: cooking, sewing, cleaning, and always wondering, "Is she going to kill me today? Is she pretending to be nice so that I'm easier to eat?"

But two weeks passed peacefully. The woman grew to like her strange-looking new friend, whose frightening face hid a gentle heart. Yet she missed her other friends, so at last she said, "I really must go home now. Everyone will be worried."

"Yes, indeed. You must go. Thank you so much," said the yamanba. "I have only a small gift, but it will last for a long time. Please take it and remember me, your new friend." Then she gave a piece of splendid golden brocade to the old woman.

"I will promise always to watch over your village," added the yamanba, "since you were so kind to me. And do come to visit, if you can. Now hurry, son, take my friend home and return right away."

With a smile, the woman left on the baby's back and in minutes reached her village. But suddenly, she heard the sad sounds of a death service.

"I wonder who has died?" she said. As she neared her own home, the sound of chanting grew louder and louder.

"What is wrong?" cried the woman through her door.

"Ah, the poor woman who lived here has died. She was eaten by that horrible yamanba," sobbed some voices. The woman opened her door and saw all the villagers sitting and crying.

"Ahhh! You should be dead! Leave us in peace, you ghost!" screamed one man.

"Go away! You must be that dreadful yamanba pretending to

be our friend," cried another neighbor.

"I am not a yamanba or a ghost. And I certainly am not dead," declared the woman, rather annoyed. But people still stared in fright right at her.

"Come, feel my bones. There's nothing wrong with me," she said, and soon her friends gathered round, touching her, much relieved to find her well.

"And there is no horrible yamanba, just a lonely one," explained the woman as she told her story. Then she unrolled the cloth and cut and cut, giving every family in the village a piece of the golden brocade. Finally, there was almost nothing left of the cloth and she was tired, so she slept, pleased and peaceful in her own home. In the morning, she almost shouted in surprise. For the golden brocade was big again, as if no one had touched it.

Many family treasures were stitched from that endless cloth, delighting the villagers. To show their thanks, they made some fresh mochi and, all together, took them up the mountain. The yamanba received them with a smile, and proudly showed off her baby.

From then on, the villagers often visited her mountaintop home. And when there was any problem in the village, the people said, "Oh, we won't worry. Our good friend the yamanba will take care of us."

And she did. So they say.

Himsuka

INDIA

Harmony demands a just ruler who governs with wisdom. Across Asia, there are many stories of kings who valued justice over even their own lives. In some Indian kingdoms, a bell was raised in a city for anyone to ring if a wrong had been done. Elsewhere in Asia, secret royal inspectors often searched for injustice. In this tale from North India, a young prince illustrates true justice using a popular Indian storytelling technique—the story within a story.

Once in India there lived a wise king with three fine sons. When his hair grew lighter than the white heron's feathers, he wished to go live simply in the forest, to pray and prepare for his next life. Yet before he left, he needed to choose his successor. Since all three of his sons were honest and good, it was hard to know who should be king. He decided to question them before making his choice.

One day he gathered them together and said, "My sons, suppose that I had a best friend, and to this friend I told important secrets about the kingdom. Then I found that he had betrayed my trust and told my secrets. What should I do?"

The first son spoke at once. "Father, since you are the king, if that friend gave away the kingdom's secrets, he must be put to death."

"Yes, father," agreed the second son. "Even though he was your friend, he was not worthy of your trust and he endangered the kingdom. He must be killed."

"Father," said the third son slowly. "If he truly gave away valuable secrets which would hurt the kingdom, he should die. But before punishing him, I would be absolutely certain of his guilt."

"What do you mean, my son?" asked his father.

"Well, to answer, let me tell you a little story," replied the son. Then he started ...

"Once there was a wise king like yourself, Father. He ruled his kingdom well and he had one best friend, a bird named Himsuka. This bird was no ordinary bird; he could speak, reason, and sing so sweetly. The two were always together. During the day, the bird talked happily, perched on the king's shoulders. At night, the bird slept on a silk cloth nestled next to him.

"One day, however, Himsuka looked out from the marble palace and saw wild birds flying freely. He suddenly wished to soar in the sky, to play on tall trees. As he thought of the world beyond the royal walls, he remembered his parents and felt most homesick.

"'My friend,' the king said just then, 'why do your eyes look so pained and your wings seem so weary?'

"'Sir,' answered Himsuka, 'you are indeed my best friend, and I love living here with you. But I miss my parents all of a sudden. I long to fly back to my forest home once again.'

"'Dearest companion,' said the king, 'I would not keep you from your mother and father. But I will miss you very much. Leave, if you must, but only for a short time. Hurry home to me, I beg you.' Himsuka promised to be back shortly, then stretched his wings and raced home.

"His parents were delighted to see him. He spent a wonderful week talking, singing bird songs, hearing bird tales, playing with his old friends. But at last it was time to return.

"'My son,' said his father, 'we will miss you, yet we know you must go. And since the king has been so kind, you should bring him a gift. But what is good enough to give a king?' Bird heads tipped in thought until the mother suddenly cried, 'The fruit of youth!'

"'Is there such a thing?' asked Himsuka. 'He surely would welcome it.'

"'I know where that precious fruit grows. I will try to bring one,' said Himsuka's father and off he flew. On toward a high mountain peak he journeyed without rest. At the top of the mountain he saw the wondrous tree, but guarded by many *rakshasa* monsters. He waited until he heard their snores thundering round the tree. Then he dove down, picked a golden fruit, and returned with it.

"'Take great care, my son,' he said, giving the fruit to Himsuka. Himsuka bid farewell and began to fly back. But it was late; he was soon tired. He saw a tree and decided to rest. Gently, he placed the fruit inside a hollow in the trunk, then wrapped his wings round himself and closed his eyes. As he slept, though, a poisonous snake crept up to the fruit and bit it. The taste didn't please him and he left, but his deadly gift remained. Hours later, when the sun smiled, Himsuka awoke, and flew on eagerly. At the palace, he gave the fruit to the king, telling him what it would bring.

"'Dear Himsuka,' said the king, 'what a wonderful gift. I must eat it right away.' But as he lifted the fruit to his mouth, an advisor suddenly stopped him.

"'Sir,' said the man, 'this is a great occasion. You must not eat the fruit alone. You must invite others to celebrate your grand fortune and to honor your dear friend.' The king agreed and several days later, he entered a throne room adorned with carpets of flowers, lit by hundreds of oil lamps. As Himsuka perched proudly on the king's shoulders and crowds of guests watched, the fruit was brought in upon a silken pillow. The king brought the fruit to his lips. Yet again he was stopped.

"'Wait, sir,' said another advisor. 'Even though this fruit is from your best friend, it must be tested for poison.' Then he cut a piece of the fruit and threw it to a crow on the windowsill. Eagerly the crow ate. And in moments, he fell dead.

"'What?' cried the king in a great rage. He turned to Himsuka who looked terribly upset and confused. 'You would kill me? You evil creature.' Then he grabbed the bird and with one violent twist, he broke the bird's neck and threw the body on the floor.

"'Remove that worthless bird, then bury this cursed fruit far away,' he commanded and left the room. Himsuka's body was tossed on the garbage, but his gift grew into a great tree with beautiful fruit. It was called the tree of death, and was guarded day and night.

"Now, in that city lived a very old couple. The two had no children, no relatives, no friends left alive. They had little money, were sick, and weary of life. One night, the old woman said to her husband, 'Let us eat a fruit of death and leave this dreadful world.' Her husband agreed, so that night he crept past the guard and stole a fruit. The two lay down upon their mats. Quietly, they shared the fruit, prayed a final prayer, bid each other farewell, and soon were very still.

"Hours later, in a red dawn rich with bird cries, the woman awoke. She looked around at what seemed to be her old hut. But next to her was not her old husband. Instead, she saw a handsome young man.

"'Could he be a god?' she wondered. Then suddenly he opened his eyes and saw a lovely young woman.

"'I must be in heaven,' he thought. 'Yet it looks like my home.' The two started to talk and realized what had happened. They rushed to the palace to tell the king about the precious life-giving fruit.

"'Ah, what did I do?' cried the king, who thought every day still of Himsuka. 'I killed my best friend without making sure of his guilt. What a terrible, terrible mistake.' And that king lived the rest of his days with remorse and sorrow.

"So, father," finished the youngest son, "that is why I say you must be sure before you act. If you feel you must punish an unworthy friend, then at least be positive of his guilt."

The old king looked at his three sons with love, then told them his clear choice. The youngest son was soon crowned the next ruler, and he led the kingdom with wisdom and compassion.

O-sung and Han-um

KOREA

A series of legends and tales has been woven around these two famous friends who really lived in sixteenth-century Korea. The ondol *floor mentioned is a most ingenious device using sets of flues underneath the floor to warm a room. Traditionally the floor was of thick oiled paper and the heat source was a kitchen fire. Today's floors may be concrete in modern highrises, but the technique is still widely used.*

One day, when O-sung was five years old, his father came home and his face grew stern. His lovely, new ondol floor, which would give such nice heat in the winter, was pierced with holes. He called to his son.

"Who made these holes?" he asked.

"Sir," said the boy, "when I wished to take a nap here, a silly flea kept on disturbing me, so I chased it with a drill."

Amused but still annoyed, the father asked, "And did you catch the flea?"

"Of course, father," replied a smiling O-sung.

"Well, even so, you must be punished for spoiling this new floor," his father said sternly.

"But sir," said O-sung, "it is not my fault that the flea came into the room."

His father could not help laughing as he said, "We shall see."

The next morning, he pointed to a grand wooden chest and told O-sung: "Since you can catch a flea with a drill, by tonight you must tell me how many rice grains are inside this or you will be punished."

O-sung looked at the huge chest so full of rice and felt very sad. Yet before he could protest, his father left. When his best friend Han-um came over, O-sung looked most upset.

"Why are you so gloomy?" asked Han-um. When he heard the problem, he simply laughed. "Come play and have fun now. We'll worry about that later."

O-sung trusted Han-um totally, so he happily played and forgot his trouble. Hours and hours later, though, as the sun went down, he grew nervous.

"Han-um," he said. "Father will soon be home. What should we do?"

"Bring me a good-sized cup," said Han-um. O-sung came running with a cup and Han-um continued, "Now fill the cup with rice and count the grains."

"There are two hundred and twenty," said O-sung soon, beginning to understand.

"Good," said his clever friend. "All we need to do now is to see how many cups are in the chest, then multiply." Happily, the boys measured the cups of rice, finding eighty in all. They finished all their calaulations well before O-sung's father returned.

When he came in, he asked at once, "How many grains? Tell me now or you must be punished."

"Seventeen thousand, six hundred," said O-sung proudly.

With a look of surprise and disbelief, his father asked, "Are you quite certain?"

"Yes, father," O-sung replied. Then he told him how his best friend had helped him. The father was well pleased with both of the boys, who knew the value of friendship and clear thinking. Instead of a punishment, they received some lovely rice balls as a treat, along with several fine books to study!

The Race

MALAYSIA

Once in Malaysia, a drongo bird perched lazily on a branch and watched a small snail below him.

"You are too slow, little one," he cried with a laugh. "I am thankful that Allah made me strong and fast."

"I may be small, but I accept what Allah gave me," replied the snail.

"You talk too proudly for a silly little snail," said the bird. "Are you challenging what I say?"

"No," said the snail. "But you are insulting me. So perhaps I must challenge you."

"Since you talk so loud, I wonder if you're strong enough to race me," the bird sang out. "Let us follow this stream to its source. If I finish first, you must guard my garden. If by some chance you win, I will watch yours."

"I agree," said snail. "But I need a little time to practice." So they set the date for one week later and the bird flew away, laughing. Quickly, the snail gathered many, many snails together.

"Dearest friends and family," he said, "the drongo bird, who is sometimes too proud, challenged me to a race up the stream. I go much too slowly to win by myself. But if you all help, we can win together. Before the race begins, please see that you are spread out along the stream, but hidden from sight. When the bird calls out, let only the snail right in front of him answer. I will hide just over the finish line to win, with your help."

The day of the race dawned early and warm. The bird flew proudly to the stream, ready to win an easy race.

"Snail, are you set to lose?" he teased.

"Perhaps," said a snail's voice. "But are you?"

"Never, never," answered the bird. "How could I lose to

such a useless little creature. Hurry and start. I have other things to do today."

At a signal, the two set off. The bird flew gracefully ahead. He looked back over his shoulder and called out happily, "Hey snail, where are you now?"

To his surprise, a voice replied ahead of him, "I'm right here." The bird flew even faster and then cried, "Now you must be so far behind, snail." But again, a voice just ahead of him shouted, "I'm right here. Hurry up." Flapping his wings faster than ever in his life, the bird raced on, calling, "Good-bye, snail." Yet once again, he was answered by a voice in front, not behind, "I'm winning, bird."

"Never," cried the bird, flying furiously until he was almost to the finish line.

"Now I won," he cried. But a small voice right in front of him answered, "What took you so long? I've been here for quite some time. I won, you lost. Remember that Allah is powerful and that each of his creatures deserves respect, no matter how small. Now go guard my garden."

The drongo bird's heart was still beating too fast, and his head flopped down on his chest. He stared at snail below him, so little he could hardly be seen.

"How could such a tiny thing beat me?" he wondered. But the result of the race seemed quite clear. So off he flew to snail's garden. And even now you can hear him call, "Auh, auh," as he watches the garden. As for snail, he and his kind lived happily from then on, working well together no matter what the problem.

4

Filial Piety and Respect for Elders

Don't take the straight path, or the winding one;
Take the path your ancestors have taken.

—**Cambodian proverb**

This saying echoes sentiments shared by many Asians who pay great respect to their parents, elders, and forebears. Getting older is not something to fight forever, as it can be in the U.S., and elders often live with families who prefer that to the nursing homes they read of in the West.

Traditionally in China, the twenty-four classic anecdotes of filial piety inspired many; and today, tales of sons and daughters who serve, obey, and help their parents still are shared. Even after death, in various Asian cultures, the family elders are honored in ceremonies on the anniversary of their death or during certain festivals.

In many Asian homes, pictures of deceased parents and grandparents are placed on a small altar or hung high on walls, and offerings are made in their behalf. The worship of ancestors and the wish to be near and to honor their graves is especially strong in lands influenced by Confucian thought.

Village of the Bell

Korea

A great emphasis is placed in Korea on filial piety; both stories and proverbs encourage proper conduct. Here is a very old version of such a tale, coming from the rich and artistic Silla Dynasty (57 B.C.E.–935 C.E.).

Long ago in the reign of King Heungduk-wang, the 42nd king of Silla, there lived an old woman whose hair was the color of onion roots. She lived with her kind son, his wife whose heart was as fine as brocade, and a little grandson who made them all forget their worries. The young couple cared for the older woman with great devotion, giving her the warmest seat in the winter, and the coolest in hot summer. Her son even walked miles to a village near the sea simply to buy the fish that she so loved.

The wife then slowly cooked the fish to perfection and served it with care. But the grandmother just gave most of it to her beloved grandson. The couple watched and worried about her health. They hid their son at mealtimes, and urged the mother to finish her fish. But she somehow managed always to hide some for the little boy she loved.

After a while, the son sadly told his wife, "I am sorry to see my mother growing weak and pale while our son is blooming in health. You know what they say—we may always have another child. But I will never have another mother. I am afraid that tomorrow we must remove our son forever, for only then will my mother grow in strength again."

His wife stared at the ground as her heart struggled against the teachings she knew so well. Then early the next morning, the two went up a nearby hill. The wife held her sleeping son; the husband carried a shovel. They found a good place for a grave and the man began to dig. Suddenly, he hit something which sang out. He dug more quickly in the ground and found a bell, a simple stone bell, with the finest sound.

"Husband," said the wife joyfully, "this must be a sign from the heavens. Please let us spare our son today and see what the bell brings."

Her husband eagerly agreed and they ran home, carrying both the bell and the boy. They hung the bell in front of their small house and listened happily whenever the wind made it ring. It was such a wondrous sound, as clear as a mountain stream, as joyful as a wild duck nearing the sea. All who heard the sound stopped, listened hungrily, then smiled secretly for hours after.

One day, the bell's song flew in the breeze, light as a dragonfly's wing, right to the palace. The king himself heard it. He marveled at the sound and sent servants to seek its source. They soon returned with the bell, the man, and his story. The king was well pleased to hear of the man's filial piety—of his devotion to his mother. Rich farmlands were given to the man so that no one in the family would ever be hungry. Then the king renamed the man's village, calling it "Chong-dong," the village of the bell, for all to remember that a devoted heart may move even heaven itself.

The family lived well from then on, and the village prospered. Now all of this happened hundreds of years ago, so all that remains of the bell today is the sound of its story, for you to pass on.

The King Who Hated the Old

LAOS

There are several different kinds of "abandoning the old" stories across Asia. In one type, the hidden elder manages to help by solving a riddle. In another, a man decides not to abandon his parent after listening to his own child.

Once in Laos, there lived a king who ruled with the wisdom of his many years, surrounded by elders who advised him well. But his son thought him foolish to keep so many older people around.

"Father, why do you listen to those silly old men?" he asked often. "Look at their white heads and their slow walks. They are useless."

The king tried to show his son that the elders had much to share, but the son just laughed and waited, knowing that when he became king, things would change. After a while, his father grew very ill and left this world. As soon as the death ceremonies were finished, the young man was crowned king. He immediately sent out his royal orders.

"All the elders in the kingdom are no longer needed. They shall be taken to distant hills and left there."

With great sorrow, his subjects obeyed the cruel command. Sons carried fathers, daughters led mothers, and many tears were shed as the elders were abandoned far from home.

In the palace, not one older advisor was left. The king brought in bright young faces and strong young bodies. One of his youthful advisors, though, found it impossible to obey the king's harsh orders.

"You have been so good to me for so many years," he sighed to his father. "How can I forget?" So he hid his father in the space under their house.

Soon after that, a messenger came from a powerful neighboring ruler and addressed the king.

"I hold here a stick from a young forest tree," he said. "Within seven days you must tell me which end of the stick comes from the higher part of the tree. If you fail, my king shall conquer your land and make you his slave."

As soon as the messenger left, the king summoned his advisors, saying, "You are all young and quick-witted. This problem should be simple. Bring me the answer tomorrow."

Everyone rushed out eagerly. But when the rooster crowed the next morning, some very tired advisors came in. No one had the answer.

"Look again at this stick," ordered the king. "Then hurry. One of you must be able to solve this riddle." But the next morning as well, there was no solution to be shared. Every day, the advisors came in with the same, sad news while their faces looked daily more worried.

The sun rose and set again and again until only one day remained. That night, as usual, the young advisor gave rice and vegetables to his father.

"My son," said the father, "why is your face as troubled as the monsoon cloud?"

"Because we will soon hear the sounds of war, father," replied the son, telling him about the messenger's challenge.

"How simple that is," said the father with a laugh. "Do not worry, but do this tomorrow." And he gave his son careful instructions. The next morning, the son ran into the throne room. Great shadows sat on all of the faces. The royal messenger was about to leave and soon the country would prepare to fight. The king, seeing the young man's smile said, "You look full of hope. When no one else could find the answer, did you?"

"Yes, indeed," he replied. "Please bring me a large bowl of water and I will give our reply." Water was brought and the king watched, most curious. The young man took the stick and placed it in the water. One end of it immediately sank down, while the other end stayed up.

"There," said the young advisor. "The end which is higher now came from the upper part of the tree. The other end, further down in the water, came from the lower part."

The messenger watched and listened. He looked carefully

at the young man, then spoke, "You have answered well and saved your land. I leave you now in peace." With a bow, he left as the king turned to the young man.

"Tell us how you found the answer when no one else could?" he asked.

"Your majesty," said the young man, "I must first admit that I disobeyed your royal command. I could not abandon my father. I kept him hidden in my home. He alone gave me the answer." The advisor then stood still, ready to accept his punishment. Silence as pure as the lotus grew in the room.

"You were correct," declared the king finally. "And I was very, very wrong. Years bring experience and wisdom not found in youth. We must have the elders to help teach us." He turned to his guards and spoke, "Go quickly. Tell everyone to bring back all who were abandoned." The men ran eagerly to spread these welcome words.

With great rejoicing, the elders returned to the kingdom. Flowers rained down as dancers danced and drummers beat a greeting. In the streets, in the homes, in the palace from that day on, the elders again shared their wisdom. And thus, all was well in the land.

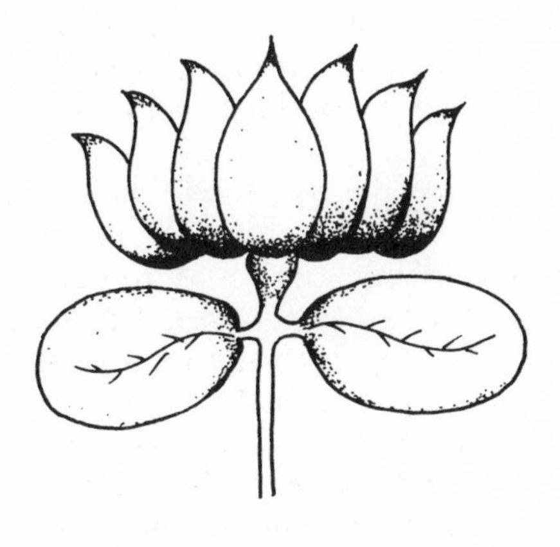

Bánh Dày, Bánh Chu'ng

VIETNAM

This popular story of New Year rice cakes helps Vietnamese children remember an important value still in Vietnam. In different versions, the meanings of the shapes may vary somewhat, but they usually nourish respect for the ancestors, and for the simple goodness of rice.

Once in Vietnam, there lived a very wise old king. After years of hard work, he knew he would soon leave this world. Since he had many sons, he announced one day that a contest would decide the next ruler.

"My sons," he said when they stood before him, "I may die soon without warning, so I must choose the next king by giving you a problem to solve. New Year approaches, the time to present the best offerings to our respected ancestors. Thus I will make king the one who can find the most excellent food to honor them."

Immediately, the different sons set off in different ways seeking food wondrous enough to win the contest. Some went to the seas; others hunted through the woods. Each was confident that he would become king—all except for the youngest son.

"How can I find the best food?" he wondered. "I am too young to go far away searching. What shall I bring?" He thought and thought and at last went to sleep, sad and discouraged. But in his sleep he had a dream. A god appeared to him.

"My son," he said, "the best food is one which everyone loves and eats—sticky rice. And the good deeds of our ancestors are as great as the heavens and the earth. So make good sticky rice into two fine shapes to honor the ancestors: a round cake to show the heavens, and a square one to stand for the earth."

In the morning the boy awoke very excited and confident. He had some good sticky rice pounded well, then shaped the rice flour into two rice cakes, wrapped them with leaves, and steamed them. One was like a circle and he called it Bánh Dày, while the square one he named Bánh Chu'ng. Days later, with a smile, he took his rice cakes before the king's high throne.

Magnificent smells swirled through the air as his brothers brought rich soups, rare fish and mushrooms, thin and thick noodles in spicy sauces. The king nibbled and tasted a little from each dish.

"These are all very fine," he said. "But which one is truly the best?"

Just then, his youngest son came up.

"Father, please try these cakes now," he said with a bow. The king stared at the very plainlooking, white rice cakes while the other princes laughed.

"How can this be the best food? It is only rice. And why is it so strangely shaped?" he asked.

"Father, my rice cakes are made from rice since the simplest food can also be the best. Everyone can enjoy rice, whether rich or poor. And the cakes are shaped to help us learn. The round shape stands for the heavens, the square shape for the earth itself. Both of these are to be offered to the ancestors, who are as important as the heavens and the earth."

The king listened to his wise son. He tasted the rice cakes with both mind and tongue. He was well pleased.

"I have found the best ruler," he said at last to all those gathered. Soon after, the boy became king, and his rule was rich in both wisdom and simple kindness to all.

The Wild Pigeon

JAPAN

In Asia, stories of all types remind people of their filial duties. Some are funny or clever, and some are more poignant as wayward or selfish children discover their mistakes too late.

Once in Japan there lived a little boy who never obeyed his mother. In fact, he loved to do just the opposite of everything she said. If she said, "Sit down," he stood up. If she said, "Go outside," he stayed in. And when she said, "Please eat," he shut his mouth.

The poor woman tried her best. She soon learned to say the opposite of what she wanted. That worked well, but it took a lot of thinking. Carefully, with many struggles, she raised her child. When he was old enough to care for himself, she grew ill and soon was about to die.

Now, the mother was very eager to be buried in a good place so that her spirit would be content and helpful. Behind her home was a hill that looked out at the sea. To be buried on top of it, sheltered by kind trees, would be just perfect.

"But if I tell my son to bury me at the top," she thought, "he will bury me at the bottom, right near the beach. That would be terrible, for the waves would attack the grave and the sun would burn it. So I must trick him a little."

She called to her son and carefully said, "My boy, soon I shall leave this world. Take good care of yourself and always feel my love. Now I must ask one favor. Please see that I am buried at the bottom of the hill, right near the ocean. Please, please, promise not to bury me at the top of the hill."

"Yes, mother, I will do as you say," said the son, feeling suddenly sad. And soon after, his mother died.

"I was a difficult child," he thought. "I never did as she

asked. I always did the opposite. So I must please her spirit and help her now. This one time, I shall do exactly as she wished." Thus he made careful preparations to bury her near the water, following her words perfectly. After a fine ceremony, the mother was buried, with great love, in exactly the wrong place.

Weeks later, it began to rain. Waves dashed up so high they almost touched the grave. Then when the sun came out, the grave had no shade or protection and it started to crack. The son worried and worried, in both rain and sun. At last, his cares grew too heavy and death took him, turning him into a wild pigeon.

On every rainy day from then on, he sadly called as he flew, "*Tetepopo, tetepopo.*" And on every sunny day from then on, he sadly called as well, "*Tetepopo, tetepopo.*" Forever after, he flew with his mournful cry, "*Tetepopo, tetepopo.*" So if you go to the sea near the beautiful city of Kanazawa even today, you may look up and see that wild pigeon. And if you hear his sad cry, you will now know why.

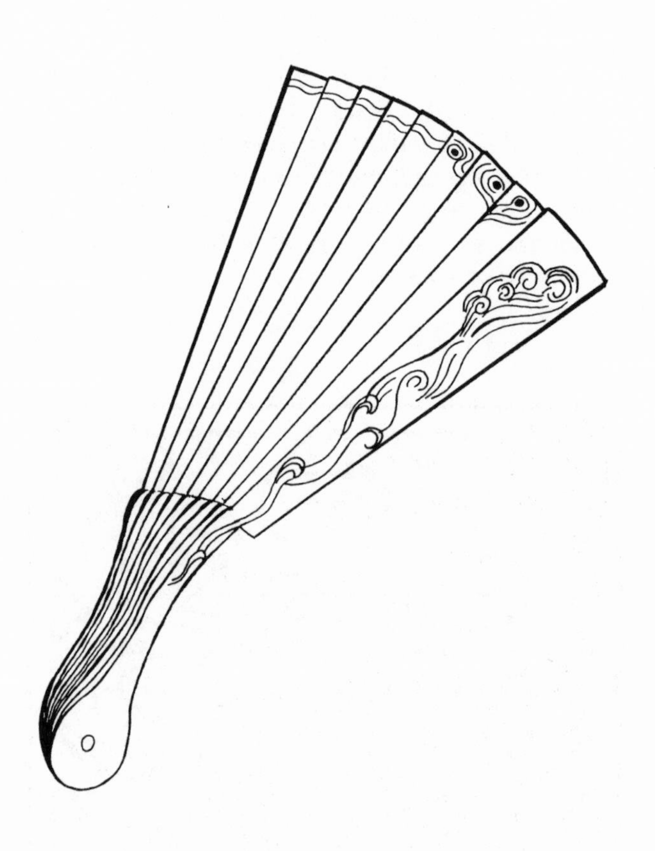

Charity and Simplicity 5

Set the bird's wings with gold
and it will never again soar in the sky.
—Rabindranath Tagore

Helping others is central to Asian life. One of Islam's five precepts is the giving of alms, while Asian Christians practice the charity which Christ taught. Buddhists and Hindus are encouraged to show compassion and to support those who ask, including monks and wandering sages. Numerous East Asian tales show kind, giving men and women rewarded for kindness. Set against them are greedy people who want too much yet get only trouble.

Hospitality as an important part of giving remains a widespread Asian value. Guests are honored and welcomed in many homes, and even the simplest meal is shared with warmth. But the traditional values that encourage a simple, giving lifestyle in some lands face new challenges from modern resource-hungry consumerism.

In Asia, as elsewhere, the challenge of the future will be to follow the prophetic words of India's Mahatma Gandhi: "The earth has enough for everyone's needs, but not enough for everyone's greeds."

Kasa Jizo

JAPAN

Here is one version of a most popular folk tale about the New Year, a favorite holiday in Japan. The story's gentle message of giving and compassion is still respected there.

Mukashi, mukashi ... Long ago, an elder couple lived simply at the foot of Kishima mountain on Kyushu island. He was a woodcarver, his fingers now curled and pained. She cooked and cleaned in slow, careful steps. Although they had little of the world's wealth, they shared a rich love, and were always ready to help others.

One year, in the middle of winter, the old woman suddenly stopped her work and said, "Husband, it will soon be New Year. But we have nothing to celebrate with, not even a coin to buy mochi. What shall we do?"

Her husband paused, wood in hand. New Year was the most important of holidays; it called for rice cakes and pine branches. The two stared sadly at the floor, hoping for an idea.

"I know what to do," she cried at last. "We'll work very hard and make some special sedge hats. Tomorrow you go to the New Year market and sell them. Surely you'll get a good sum and with that, you can buy what we need."

It was a good plan. That day and into the cold night, they sipped weak *ocha*, green tea, and worked until their frozen fingers rebelled. Three perfect hats stood ready to sell as the couple fell into a satisfied sleep. At dawn, after a meal of miso soup, the man started off. Across the mountain and through the rice fields he walked happily and soon reached the New Year market.

"*Kasa, kasa*," he called to sell his hats near those who sold pine branches for the holiday. But no one in the crowded market even stopped to look at his hats. There was too much else to buy. And soon, the sun moved overhead.

"Never mind," he told himself. "After they eat, someone will come to buy my hats." His tired voice called again and again, "*Kasaaa, Kasaaa.*" People bustled back and forth, but no one stopped, no one even glanced at the hats. And soon, the sun settled down.

"*Kasaa, Kasaa,*" whispered the old man, his throat sore. No one heard. The market was over, the streets were empty. Everyone was home now, content behind closed doors, busy preparing for a grand New Year.

With a sigh that stretched down his aching back, the man began the long walk home, *so-ro, so-ro, so-ro, so-ro.* His steps were slow, heavy with disappointment. He clutched the hats. He tried to forget what a bleak New Year it would be.

As he slipped across the rice fields, an icy rain fell, splashing cold water, *pa-cha, pa-cha.* Shivering, the man slowed and suddenly felt eyes staring through him. Close by, he saw a sad and lonely stone Tanu-kami-sama, god of the rice field. The sleet beat down on the statue as it quietly guarded the crops.

"You poor thing," sighed the man. "You will be too cold this New Year night. I wish I could help." He stood still and then remembered his hats. With a smile, he reached for one of them and placed it carefully on the statue's head. "Perhaps this will keep away the rain," he said as he bowed and walked on.

A quiet road snaked across the mountain. Higher and higher he followed it, walking slowly, *so-ro, so-ro.* Then, on the roadside, under a blanket of frozen moss, he saw a statue of the Jizo that protected children. The kind man moved close to the neglected Jizo and brushed off some of the ice.

"Ahhh," he sighed, "you, too, need to be protected tonight." He gently placed another hat on the Jizo's head, and with palms together in salute, he bid farewell. Farther along the darkened path he climbed, up and over the mountaintop.

"*Samuiiiii, samuiiiii.* It's too cold," whimpered a voice ahead of him. The man hurried toward the sound and found a tiny monkey shivering on the head of another carved stone—one shaped as Yama-no-kami-sama, the mountain god.

"Here," said the man, "use this hat to keep away the rain." He tied the last hat on the mountain god so that it sheltered the monkey as well.

"Please, Yama-no-kami-sama, keep all the little monkeys warm," pleaded the man. Then, much lighter in load and mind, he walked quickly toward home, *te-ku, te-ku, te-ku, te-ku.*

"*Tadiama*, I'm home," he sang out.

"*Okaeri nasai*," his wife replied in welcome.

"You sold all of the hats," she said with a grin. "But where are the mochi, the pickles, the pine branches? And you look so cold. Come sit by the fire, sip some ocha." As they sat around the *irori* firepit, the man rubbed his hands and slowly told her what he had done. His wife smiled warmly, *ni-ko, ni-ko.*

"What a good thing you did!" she said. "Truly, we don't need anything more for New Year. Let us drink the last of our sweet potato wine to celebrate." So the two finished the warm brew and grew sleepy. Snores soon tore through the dark as New Year dreams soothed the couple.

In the middle of the night, a work chant pushed through the walls, "*Yoi-sho, yoi-sho.*" The couple awoke, confused, for the sound seemed to be coming across the fields and right to them. They huddled together, listening as the voices came closer and closer, louder and louder, and then stopped outside their home.

"Open the door, old man," whispered the woman. "Someone is waiting out there." When he pulled the door open, three statues greeted him.

"*Domo arigato gozaimasu.* Thank you for your kindness," said the first statue, the Tanukamisama from the rice field. "Here is a rice bag which will never be empty." He handed it to the man.

"I thank you as well," said the second statue, the Jizo. "Take this money. Although there isn't much, good fortune comes with it." The Jizo handed the man a few coins.

"All the monkeys are warm now," said Yama-no-kami-sama, the third statue. "Please accept this mountain tea in return for your good-hearted act." He handed the man a few leaves of green tea. And then the three statues bumped away back up the mountain, *cho-ko, cho-ko, cho-ko, cho-ko,* while the old couple stared in amazement.

"What a strange and wonderful night,"said the woman at last and then she boiled some mountain tea. It made them pleasantly tired so they slept a fine sleep.

"*Ko-ke-kok-ko, ko-ke-kok-ko*" soon crowed the rooster to

greet the New Year day. The woman stretched, rubbed her face, then sat up in surprise. She peered at her husband, her eyes wide.

"Husband, husband." She shook him awake. "What has happened to us? I feel so strong. And you look so young." For her husband's face was now that of an eighteen-year-old.

"My wife, you look today just like the youngster I married so long ago," he said with a smile. "How can that be?" They both stared at each other and then laughed and laughed. What a fine gift the mountain god had given them—a gift of youth.

The bottomless rice bag was enjoyed as well, and the few coins were quite enough, for the couple had little need of money. From that day on, fortune wrapped her arms round them and they lived most happily for a long time.

Even today, there at the foot of Kishima mountain where once they lived, rice is still plentiful and people don't run madly after money. And every New Year morning, it is the custom to sip green mountain tea and then exclaim to those near you, "Ah, you look so young today!"

Oshimai. That is all.

Kim Sondal and the River

KOREA

Kim Sondal is a popular trickster in Korea. In this tale, he helps move wealth from greedy rich to needy workers.

Every day, tired men carried water from the Daedong river to the houses of the rich. Yet while the poor workers struggled with heavy loads, the greedy rich only wasted water, and cheated those who carried it. Thus the rich grew richer and the poor grew weaker.

One night, though, clever Kim Sondal heard the water carriers complaining.

"I can help you," he said. "I'll loan you some money now and we will play a trick. Every day when you come from the river, you will find me sitting on the riverbank. Drop a coin in front of me as you walk by."

The next morning, Kim Sondal spread out a cloth and sat near the river. As each water carrier passed, he threw a coin onto the cloth. That night, Kim Sondal secretly returned the money so that the men could throw the same coins again the next day and the next.

Day after day, Kim Sondal picked up piles of coins and soon the lazy rich men who loafed by the river began to notice. At last they asked what he was doing.

"I am collecting my tax on the river water," he replied.

"But you don't own the river," they objected.

"Yes, I do," he said. "Don't you see how the men pay me each time they take water? They know that it is mine."

Now the rich men grew more and more jealous of Kim Sondal's growing wealth. The coins on his blanket looked so inviting.

"Every night he takes home too many coins," said the rich

men to each other. "He will soon have more money than we will. Perhaps we should buy the river and then we'll get richer than ever."

And so it was decided. The rich men went to Kim Sondal as he sat counting his coins.

"We wish to buy the river so that you can relax," they said, offering him a decent price.

"Friends, I make much money from my river," replied Kim Sondal. "How can I sell it for such a small amount?" Quickly, the men talked among themselves and then raised their offer. But he still refused, so the offer went even higher. And higher. At last, after much bargaining, he sold the river for a very large sum. That night, he divided the money happily among the water carriers.

Hours later, as birds welcomed dawn, the rich men spread out a huge cloth and sat, waiting eagerly for their river money. Finally, a water carrier came. They pointed to the cloth, but the man passed right by without a pause.

"You forgot to pay for the water. It's our river now," they cried. He looked at them with the strangest expression, then shrugged his shoulders and walked on. Another man soon came carrying a load of water.

"Pay for that water," cried the rich men. "We own the river now." But the man only laughed and walked on.

Along came another carrier who did the same. And another and another. The rich men spent a long, unhappy day until at last they realized how well they'd been tricked. They returned home in anger, and the river water, precious as it was, remained free to all.

Prince Vetsandon

CAMBODIA

One of the most popular stories in Laos, Thailand, Cambodia, Sri Lanka, and Burma is the tale of Prince Vetsandon (or Vessantara, as he is widely called), the last incarnation of the Buddha before his enlightenment. During this final lifetime of preparation, the prince was known especially for his great charity. Here is an abridged Cambodian version of a major piece of world literature.

Long ago, in the kingdom of Chetador, a young prince, Vetsandon, was born ever eager to give and give. On the day of his birth, a magnificent white elephant came as well into the world. From that day, the boy and the elephant lived in royal surroundings of beauty and peace.

As he grew in years, Prince Vetsandon grew in his desire to give. He gave away his favorite toys of gold and silver easily to all who asked. When he received a chain with one hundred thousand coins from his father, he gave it at once to his nurses. One day, at the age of eight, he suddenly thought, "Until today, everything which I have given away has not been mine. I have only received it and passed it along. How I wish I could give away something truly of my own. If someone would ask, I would eagerly give my eyes, my heart, my flesh." At these thoughts of one so young, the earth quaked like a mad elephant and the sky thundered.

Vetsandon studied hard in the palace, and by age sixteen, he had mastered all sciences and arts. After that, his father arranged a fine marriage. Princess Metri became Vetsandon's kind wife, and the two were blessed with a boy, Cheali, and a girl, Kresna.

At that time, the people in the next kingdom, Chetareas, were suffering from starvation. When the rain refused to fall

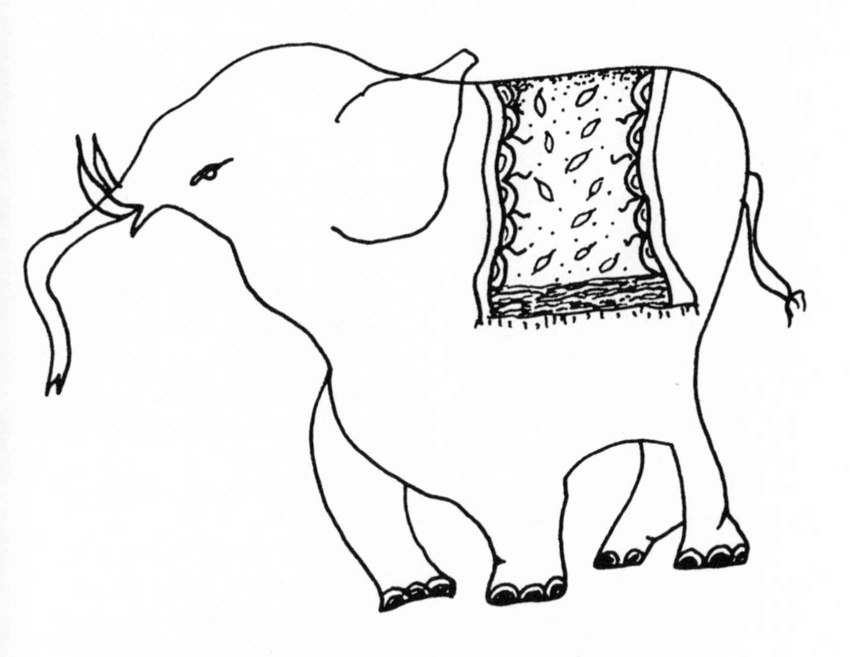

there even after their king's many vows, the people remembered the great white elephant in Vetsandon's kingdom.

"If only we had that auspicious animal, the rains would surely come," they said. "Since Vetsandon is known for his giving, let us send someone to ask. Perhaps that gracious prince will offer the blessed elephant to help us."

Days later, several priests journeyed to see Vetsandon. As soon as they asked, Vetsandon presented the elephant to them, along with the gold and gems upon it. At that moment, again, the earth quaked and the city walls trembled at such generosity.

But even as the pleased priests led the elephant away, the people in Vetsandon's city were much upset. They feared ill fortune without their elephant. With angry voices, they demanded that the prince be punished, that he leave the kingdom.

Sadly, Vetsandon's father called to his son and told him the people's wishes. Prince Vetsandon, ever respectful both to his parents and to those he ruled, agreed at once.

"Please father," he said, "give me one more day. For before I leave, I wish to give the great gift of seven hundreds." Word raced around the city and the next day, people gathered eagerly. Smiling simply, the prince gave away seven hundred elephants, seven hundred horses, seven hundred chariots, seven hundred cows, and cartloads of jewels, clothes, and objects of great worth.

The following day, he, his wife, and their children set out for the forest in a chariot. But they were met by four men rushing to the city.

"Is the great prince still offering gifts?" they asked eagerly.

"Friends," said Vetsandon with real pain, "you are too late. But wait, I will find something for you." He happily untied the four horses of the chariot and gave one to each man. Just then, a priest, too, came seeking wealth, and he received the chariot. Vetasandon and Metri walked on, carrying their children. They stayed that evening in a neighboring city where the people wished Vetsandon to remain and rule.

"Dear friends, I thank you," replied Vetsandon gently. "But I must follow my father's wishes and go to the forest." Thus, after a pleasant night, the four walked on into the woods.

There they lived simply and well. As the children played with the deer and watched frogs in the lotus pond, their mother collected forest fruit and roots. In the evenings, they shared a meal with the forest creatures, then slept in peace.

One day, though, when Metri was away, an old man named ChuChuk came with a most terrible request. ChuChuk's young wife had threatened to leave him if he didn't provide servants for her. Knowing of Vetsandon's great and giving nature, ChuChuk decided to come ask for his children.

"If you are truly as generous as they say, then give me your children to be my servants," he said, standing before Vetsandon. Although Vetsandon felt great love for his children, he was preparing for a very special role. He needed to give without question, to live without any attachment. Only then would he be ready for his incarnation as the Buddha—a lifetime which would bring comfort and help to so many. To reach that noble goal, he had to offer his children to ChuChuk.

But his children were scared, hiding in the lotus pond. ChuChuk had trouble finding them and spoke sharply to

Vetsandon, "Is this your giving? Your words mean nothing."

"Dear children, do come," Vetsandon called softly to them. Hearing their father and respecting his words, they came out.

"Father, please let us wait until mother returns, to say good-bye," they begged. Yet ChuChuk, that heartless man, had come during the day just to avoid Metri, for he feared her anger.

"They must come now," he demanded and Vetsandon agreed, fixing a price for each child's freedom, should anyone ask. Not wishing to argue with the father they loved, the two let cruel ChuChuk tie them and take them roughly away.

Seeing his children go in this way greatly upset Vetsandon. With his heart quaking, he stepped into his hut, to calm himself, to control the anger which suddenly made him wish to run and bring them back.

Bravely the children walked on, but then seeing a chance to escape, they fled back to their father. They begged to stay, but ChuChuk again demanded them harshly from Vetsandon. And again, an anguished Vetsandon had to make his children go.

"Then give mother our toys—the little horse, the elephant, the others—to help her, for she will be very, very sad," cried the boy while ChuChuk pulled them away.

As the sound of their sobs faded, Vetsandon tried to calm his mind, tried to stop his grief. He sat in silence for hours until Metri returned, very late, from the forest. Her arms full, she stopped in a clearing near their home, puzzled.

"Where are the children tonight?" she wondered. "They always run right to me here, to greet me, to tell me of their day, their play." In a worried silence she walked up to her husband.

"Are the children trying to trick me?" she asked. "Are they hiding in the forest? Where are they?"

At first there was no reply. She asked again, more worried, and at last Vetsandon told what he had done. At that, she fainted upon the ground. When she opened her eyes again her grief was so great she wished only to die. Yet she knew that her husband was not an ordinary man. Thus, with pain, she accepted his decision, for she felt it would help so many in the future. But to herself, she made a vow to eat only one meal a day and to sleep upon the stony ground until they returned.

At this moment, in the heavens, the gods looked down

and decided to give one final and terrible test to Vetsandon. They wished to see if he could give up even the wife whom he loved so much. Taking the form of a priest, one of the gods came to Vetsandon's door.

"I am growing older," he said. "I have need of someone to help me, to be with me." He looked at Metri, and Vetsandon now faced his last test—to allow his lifemate, his dearly beloved, to leave. Metri, in her wisdom and understanding, said not a word as Vetsandon bowed his head and agreed to this impossible request.

At that moment, when he gave away this final love, gave up his last earthly attachment, the skies shook and the mountains roared. Huge waves crashed in the sea and fish jumped out of the waters, knowing that a great event had taken place. The heavens, well pleased, rained down flowers upon him. And since Vetsandon had passed this final test, Metri was sent happily back to her husband.

Meanwhile, ChuChuk walked on with the children. But the gods were watching and protecting the two. At night, they came down and tenderly cared for and comforted the children as ChuChuk slept. And they caused him to wander in confusion not to his own city but instead to Vetsandon's old kingdom.

There, word reached the children's grandparents, who were overjoyed to see the two. They gladly paid for the children's freedom and then at a feast to celebrate, the greedy ChuChuk ate so much that he burst.

By this time, the people of the kingdom had realized their mistake. Again, they approached the old king, now seeking Prince Vetsandon's return.

With great joy, the king agreed to his heart's dearest wish. Soon, thousands of flowers covered the path to the forest. Cooling drinks and sweets were placed along the road. A grand procession moved joyfully towards the woods as sounds of drums and lutes raced ahead. Elegant dancers sculpted the air with their hands, scattering scented petals as they walked. Thousands of elephants shining in golden robes swayed gracefully near thousands of chariots carrying nobles and saints of the land.

In the distance, Vetsandon and Metri saw the dust of so many feet and feared an army's attack. As the huge throng came closer, the couple recognized the friendly banners and faces from their homeland. They waited eagerly as the procession neared and the king approached.

"My son, please come back and rule again as you should," begged Vetsandon's father, stepping up to them. Vetsandon asked first for word of his children, and suddenly the two youngsters raced to their parents, who held them with great joy.

Vetsandon and Metri then put on royal silks and jewels as easily as they had taken the forest robes of bark. Like gods from the heavens covered in glory, the royal couple returned to rule with wisdom and compassion. Vetsandon continued his generous ways until at last he left this world. And after his death, because of his limitless charity and perfection, he was born again as the noble prince who at last became the great Lord Buddha.

Too Much

PHILIPPINES

King Ramos and his wife were greedy and mean-spirited rulers long ago in the beautiful Philippines. Although they had wealth enough to end hunger forever on their island, they used their treasure only on themselves. The queen dressed in the most exquisite silks; the king had weapons heavy with gold; their palace was covered with costly carvings. And they loved to give dinners for the richest people in the kingdom—meals with so much food that cartloads of leftovers could be thrown away as waste, to prove their wealth.

Once in the heat of summer, they decided to host a grand dinner outside under a full moon. Sparkling lights greeted their guests along with piles of rice, the sweetest fruits, and the smells of fine sauces.

As the guests sat enjoying the feast, a poor, ragged woman came wandering in. She went from table to table seeking a little rice. But no one gave even a grain. Instead they mocked her. One of the guests picked up a spoon and tossed it at the woman. Then another guest tried the same.

"Let us all throw spoons at the old hag!" cried the queen, always eager for an amusing game. "Whoever hits her on the head wins a prize." At once, spoons flew through the air as the woman stumbled from side to side, trying to avoid them. The guests laughed when the spoons hit her knees, her arms, her back. They tried even harder to hit her head.

All of a sudden, there was a great flash of light and a lovely woman in white stood where the old one had been.

"A curse on you all!" she cried. "You are too greedy and cruel to live as humans. From now on, you will be scorned by those you have scorned."

She disappeared and spoons flew again through the air.

But now they hit the guests, the king, the queen. As they ran to escape, their fine silks turned into soft fur on their bodies and their arms grew suddenly longer. They stared at each other. They saw hairy, crumpled echoes of human faces in front and in the back, bottoms red from the spoons.

Much ashamed, those greedy people, those who would not share, ran to hide in the forest and there they stayed as the first monkeys of that land.

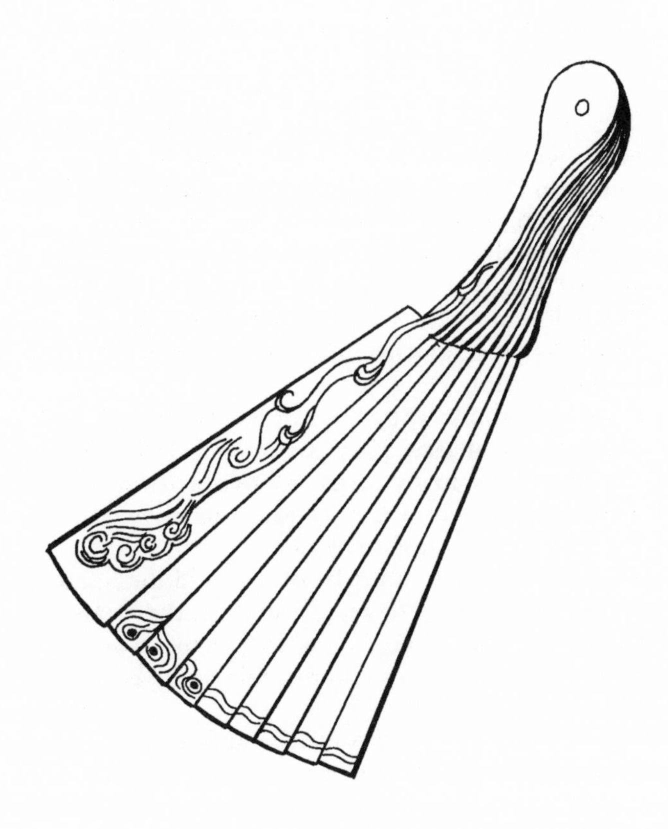

The Visit

INDIA

Giving hospitality is an important value in Asia, but how it is given varies. In Japan, it may be warmly extended after one has been properly introduced. In India, less formal hospitality is apparent in this true story from one of my friends.

Once a couple went to visit the city of Ayodhya in North India. With them they carried a letter from their friends, the Rastogi family in Delhi. It was addressed to a brother who lived in Ayodhya, asking him to take good care of the visitors. The couple arrived in the evening after a hot, crowded train ride and debated what to do. The city was new to them and they had only a letter with an address, but no telephone number to call. They showed the name on the envelope to several rickshaw drivers at the train station.

"I know the family. They live not too far away. Climb in," said an older driver at last. They got into his rickshaw and he started pedaling. After many turns and twists down small lanes and large, they arrived at a house, paid the driver, and introduced themselves, presenting the letter.

"Please come in. You must be tired," said the homeowner as his wife brought refreshing tea. Gratefully, the weary couple sipped tea, bathed, then shared a meal of *chappati* and *dal* with their new hosts. Feeling very comfortable and well taken care of, they enjoyed a fine sleep.

In the morning after a leisurely breakfast, the man of the house spoke. "Now that you have rested and are feeling stronger, I will take you to the right place."

The two from Delhi looked at each other in surprise as their host continued. "You see, our name is Rastogi, but we have no relatives in Delhi. We do not know your friends there, and we never heard of their brother here. Last night, though, it was late and you were tired. We did not want to upset you or send you away. We were happy to offer what little we could. Now, this morning, I have made inquiries and found the correct house."

With a smile, he led the very bewildered but thankful couple to the right Rastogi family. There they stayed for several days, and the week ended as nicely as it began, thanks to the unquestioning warmth of Indian hospitality.

Hard Work and Study 6

Behind the mountain of sacrifices lies the valley of success.
—Filipino proverb

Across Asia, the importance of study, learning, and diligent work is often emphasized. Students in various Asian countries study hard to succeed in the crucial examinations which determine who gets into the best universities, and thus gets the best jobs. Numerous afterschool "cram schools" or tutors help students prepare for tests still based on much memorization.

Exams were most important earlier in China, Korea, and Vietnam as ways to determine official standing. Tales of such difficult exams and of the dedication which they demanded are still shared. Today, as in the past, mothers do much to support such study. Yet while scholarship is respected, common sense is admired as well. An Indian *Panchatantra* fable makes a lesson of the foolish scholars who revived a lion, just to show off their learning. This rhyme, in the fable, underlines the moral.

Scholarship is less than sense,
Therefore seek intelligence.
Senseless scholars in their pride,
Made a lion and then they died.[1]

In lands where human resources are more plentiful than natural resources, common sense includes using things carefully and learning not to waste. And in the end, hard work and common sense find their own reward, though in some religions the gods add a blessing as well.

Ondal the Fool

KOREA

A Korean proverb recalls this well-known story: Out of the rags comes a hero. General Ondal and Princess Pyongkang lived in the second half of the sixth century, but their tale is still told today.

Princess Pyongkang was a crybaby. She cried the minute she was born in long-ago Korea and did not stop. At first, people didn't mind that a royal baby cried. They tried to help her. She grew a bit older, and although she still wept, people kept quiet. But when she grew older yet and her tears still spilled, the sound became a terrible nuisance.

As her cries echoed through palace halls, her mother, the queen, felt helpless, while her father, the king, grew very annoyed.

"*Stop*," he ordered when she sobbed near him. But she would not.

"*Stop at once*," he commanded. But the tears still fell. Finally, in a great rage one day he shouted, "*If you don't stop, you will marry Ondal the fool!*"

Now this was a threat indeed. Ondal was a beggar. He was ugly. He roamed the streets in rags, selling sticks he found and hunting scraps to feed his mother. He was so foolish, people said, that when children teased him, he didn't even fight back. He just smiled softly, as if he had a secret, and walked right on.

Yet even the threat of such a terrible marriage, repeated often, did not keep the girl from weeping. Then suddenly, her years outgrew her tears and at last the cries stopped. She blossomed into a thoughtful young woman—as sweet as a melon, as pretty as a peach. When she grew old enough to be wed, her parents proudly searched the kingdom for a suitable match. Soon, with a smile, her father called for her and spoke.

"We have found a perfect husband for you. He comes from a royal family, is a skilled horseman, a scholar, and a brave warrior."

"But father," said the princess, "you told me many times that my husband would be Ondal the fool."

"You silly girl," replied the king, "I spoke only to stop your tears. A princess can never marry a beggar."

"But a king can never take back his words," she said. "If I do not marry Ondal, people will lose faith in you."

"*Stop! Stop this nonsense!*" ordered the king. Bravely, though, his daughter insisted. At last he could stand no more of her talk and sent her away thundering, "*Leave then and marry your fool!*"

While her mother wept, the princess gathered her jewels and left the palace. Her footsteps led her at sunset to a hill where Ondal gathered twigs.

In the twilight, the princess walked slowly toward him, her silk gown sweeping the earth, her wide sleeves like dragonfly wings, her eyes glowing like pearls. Ondal was surprised, then frightened.

"Who are you?" he whispered.

"I am Princess Pyongkang. I am to marry you."

"*Oh no,*" he cried. "*No noble woman would come here alone at night. You must be a ghost. Go away. Go!*" Terrified, he raced home to hide from this evil spirit.

The princess followed. She knocked upon the door, and when there was no answer, she sat next to it. All night, in the cold shadows, she pressed herself to the walls patiently waiting for the dawn. As the morning light warmed her spirits, the door opened and Ondal saw her.

"Please tell me, who are you?" he asked and she told him once again.

"Forgive my rudeness," he begged, believing her now. "But you must go. You cannot stay in this poor place. You belong in the palace."

"I belong here," she replied. "My father told me so, long ago." She insisted until at last he invited her in. She met his mother and bowed to her as a daughter-in-law. Then, in the simplest of ceremonies, the princess married the beggar.

From that day on, she lived in the hut, helping her mother-in-law and her husband. Her soft fingers now stitched rough cloth; her royal tongue tasted only food scraps. And as the days passed, she saw in her husband not an ugly fool, but a man with kind eyes, a good heart, and a clear mind. So one day, she traded her jewels for a horse, a sword, and books printed from rare woodblocks.

These she gave to Ondal, saying, "My husband, you can do great things. But you must begin to study. You are starting later than most men to learn the teachings of the wise, thus you must work even harder. And I will help."

From then on, day after day, under the sun, he rode swiftly upon his horse, perfecting the skills of a warrior. Night after night, under a pine oil light, he slowly learned to read. He worked with determination, although it was very difficult and he often grew discouraged. But the princess urged him on with her gentle smile and her trust. She told him tales of heroes and read to him words of the wise. She inspired him when he was ready to give up.

After many, many months of effort, she gazed with pride upon her husband, now a brave warrior and a man of learning. One night she said, "The great hunt at Nangnang comes soon on the third day of the third moon. You must go hunt with the warriors of Koguryo kingdom, then offer wild boar and deer to the mountains, the rivers there."

Thus he journeyed to Nangnang and hunted with such courage and skill that the king himself watched, much impressed. In the evening, he bowed before the king, who praised him and asked his name.

"Ondal, sir."

"Ondal? Surely not the fool Ondal?" said the king, much amazed. When he heard the story of his daughter's wisdom, he was well pleased and longed to see her. There was soon a grand reunion at the palace and Ondal became a general, eager to defend his land.

Many times he led his soldiers as they charged, like angry waves, against those who invaded Koguryo. Many times he won, inspiring his men. After great success in battle, he was promoted to one of the highest ranks in the palace. Then, as an honored officer, he offered to go reclaim land north of the Han river seized by a neighboring kingdom.

The king gave his blessing, the princess gave her love, and General Ondal set out. At Achasong fortress, near present-day

Seoul, he fought bravely, like a tiger. His men followed him faithfully into battle. But he was only human and all of a sudden, an arrow pierced his chest.

Ondal fell from his horse, and his blood fell on the ground. He called faintly for the princess and died, they say, with her name upon his lips. His body was placed sadly in a coffin to be returned to the capital. Yet when the soldiers tried to lift it, the coffin stayed, as if rooted. The strongest men strained and struggled, but it did not move at all.

The princess was told and came swiftly. She threw herself on the coffin and wept greater tears than ever she had as a child.

"Come, my brave and beloved husband," she cried. "Come home and rest. Truly, you have earned the peace you now shall have."

At once, the coffin seemed lighter. It was carried easily back to the palace and buried then with great ceremony and respect.

Many hundreds of years have passed since that day, but this true tale of Ondal and Princess Pyongkang is still told and retold in Korea. For it proves that love can reach across great differences, that hard work can conquer hardship, and that wisdom and courage flourish in huts as well as in royal halls.

Dividing the Property

BANGLADESH

In this version of a well-known tale, the coconut trees and the nakshi kantha *help to place it in Bangladesh. This distinctive quilt is made from several layers of used, white sari pieces stitched together. Covering it in rich embroidered detail are animal and human figures, flowering trees, and stories as well.*

Once in Bangladesh, Selim, who had little good sense, lived with his tricky older brother, Ali. After their parents died, the boys were left with their small home, a cow, several coconut trees, and a beautiful kantha quilt.

"Let us be fair," said Ali. "We must share everything that we have. We will first share the cow. You may have the front, with the mouth, which is the best part, and I shall take only the back."

Young Selim was overjoyed at his brother's generosity. Every day, he took good care of the cow, petting her fondly and feeding her nice, fresh grass. Every day, Ali did no work except to milk the cow. And, of course, he kept all of that rich milk just for himself.

Many days passed. Selim grew weaker and weaker, while Ali glowed with health. Finally one morning, a wise neighbor came to talk with Selim.

"My boy," she said, "you are looking so pale, so tired. What is the problem?"

"I don't have much to eat," he sighed.

"But I see you feeding that fine cow every day. Surely she gives enough milk for both of you boys," said the neighbor.

"Ah, yes, I suppose she does, but I don't drink it," explained Selim. "You see, my brother wanted to be fair, so we divided the cow. I get the front, which he said was the best. But it doesn't seem to give me any milk." The woman shook her head at such foolishness, then whispered something to him.

The next day, when Ali came to milk his half, Selim moved the cow's head quickly this way and that, back and forth, so that Ali couldn't get any milk from the angry animal.

"Brother, what are you doing?" he cried.

"I'm exercising the part that belongs to me," replied Selim. Ali realized at once that someone had helped his brother, so he said, "All right, Selim. From now on we'll share the cow equally. I'll help you feed her, and you'll drink half of her milk." So at last Selim enjoyed fine cow's milk.

But the next day, Ali said, "Now it is time to share the coconut trees that father left us. Since I am elder and taller, I will take the top parts and you can have the bottoms. That is the fairest way."

Selim agreed that it seemed most reasonable. Every day, Selim faithfully watered the trees, but the trunks had no coconuts for him. Every few days, Ali climbed up to his part of the trees, picked fine coconuts, then sold them in town.

One day, the wise neighbor saw Ali happily carrying coconuts to the market, while Selim sadly watered the trees.

"You must be pleased with all the coconuts on your trees," she said to Selim.

"But they don't belong to me," replied Selim. "They come from the top and that's Ali's part." So the woman whispered some more advice.

Early the next morning, Selim began to chop down a coconut tree.

"*What are you doing?*" asked Ali, running out.

"The bottoms are mine, so I'm cutting them all," replied a smiling Selim. Ali knew that, again, his brother had found help. So Ali promised to share the coconuts, too.

"Now, brother," said Ali, "there is one last item to divide—the lovely kantha made by our mother. Let us share it in this way: you use it in the daylight to admire its beauty. I will use it at night, even though it is too dark to see it."

"You are so kind, my brother," said Selim as he smiled. Every day, he gazed with pleasure at the kantha's designs. But at night, with no cover, he felt too cold and could hardly sleep. Yet next to him, Ali slept under the cloth, snoring loudly. Finally, Selim went to the neighbor, asked for help, and returned well pleased.

At noon the next day, he suddenly poured water all over the kantha, soaking it completely.

"What are you doing, fool? It will stay wet for days!" shouted Ali when he saw the watery mess.

"I can do what I wish since it's my turn now," said Selim. "So whenever it is hot, I'll cool off the kantha."

"All right, brother," said Ali with a grin. "You are becoming too clever. I'd better stop my tricks. From now on, we'll both share it at night and stay warm. And I promise never to trick you again!"

Ali kept his word, surprising both his wise neighbor and his brother. He never did trick Selim again, although perhaps he found someone, somewhere to trick instead. At last, the two brothers lived happily together, working hard and sharing both good and bad, for a long, long time.

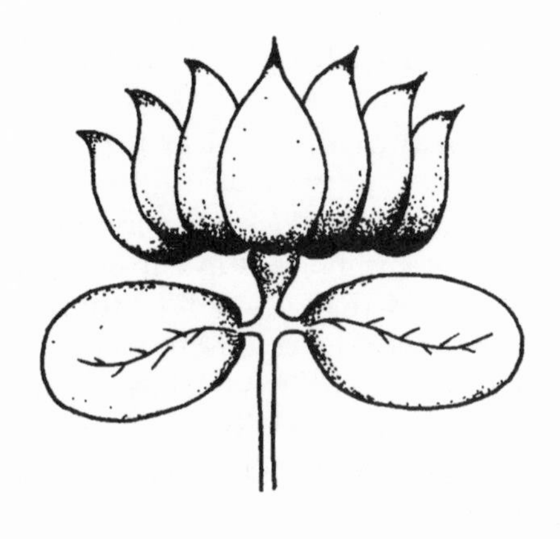

A Clever Trade

INDIA

Indians are some of the world's best recyclers. Homework papers are folded into bags, which are later recycled again; tires become well ropes, sandals, toys, and more; leaves are pinned into great disposable plates; and cloth scraps blossom into intricate bags and hangings. But new clothes are worn for the Diwali festival, which is celebrated today with glimmering lights, worship, sweets, and fireworks.

Once in India, a proud king ruled with less of wisdom and more of greed. While his subjects worked too hard, he played and gambled. Soon, the foolish king had gambled away his home, his wealth, and even his kingdom. Thus he, his son, and his son's clever wife, Shantha, had to leave their fine palace and journey to a far-off land.

There the three lived, in a tiny home with the stars for a ceiling. The men went out seeking work by day while Shantha used her wits to stretch their few coins.

"Whenever you go out," she told them, "always pick up something to bring home. It can be a stick, a stone, an old cloth piece, a large leaf, anything by the side of the road."

The men listened well, the three worked hard, and, slowly, their life improved. When the men brought home big stones, Shantha built a strong wall. When they brought home bits of cloth, she stitched a colorful bedspread. When they brought home big leaves, she pinned them together into strong plates. One day, though, all they could find was a dead black snake.

"I'm not certain what to do with this," Shantha said honestly. "But I'm sure we'll find a use for it." With a smile, she threw it up on their ragged roof.

While sweeping early the next morning, she saw a bird fly overhead, holding something bright and shiny. Suddenly, it swooped down and picked up the dead snake, leaving behind its sparkling treasure. Shantha reached up to the roof, found what was there, and hid it in the house. She waited eagerly for the men, who returned at sunset with exciting news.

"The queen's necklace has been stolen," cried her husband. "And a reward is offered to anyone who returns it." Hearing this, Shantha smiled. She reached under a mat and brought out a necklace of golden lotus leaves.

"Is this it?" she asked. The old man and his son looked fearfully at the royal treasure.

"You did not steal it, did you?" her husband asked, afraid to hear her reply. She laughed, then told them of the bird's trade. After that, they dressed as best they could and hurried to the palace. As the sun's farewell spread across the sky, they approached the guards. Moments later, they stood before the royal couple. With a bow, Shantha presented the necklace to the queen, whose face at once glowed brighter than the moon.

"Ask what you will as your reward," said the king. "Do you desire gold, gems, or fine silks?"

"No, your majesty," said Shantha. "We wish only this: on Diwali holiday, our house alone shall have light, while all else in the land must be dark."

Hearing her wish, the king grew sad. Usually that night, the palace was a blaze of bright light to welcome the Goddess Lakshmi, who gave good fortune when she came to the earth.

"You ask a difficult reward. Everyone wishes to greet the goddess on that night," he said.

"All are welcome to burn candles and lamps near our home," replied Shantha. Thus the king had to agree, and a decree was sent out with his orders.

Before Diwali, the three cleaned their house and yard most carefully. On the day of the great festival, Shantha made sweets, prepared a place for *puja* (worship), rolled cotton wicks, and dripped oil into little clay lamps. Next she let fine powder trickle through her fingers as she drew rich *rangoli* patterns upon the earth. Soon the footsteps of the goddess, along with her favorite flower, the lotus, lay like a fine carpet on the ground.

As twilight crept around Shantha, people came to light their lamps. Soon hundreds of flames danced joyfully and her house was brighter than the sun.

At that moment, the Goddess Lakshmi came from the heavens, ready to visit the palace and the many homes she yearly blessed. But darkness like a black cobra stretched over the land. There was no moon and there seemed to be no city. Confused and tired, she searched for even a small light, a simple greeting. All at once, she saw a blaze glowing far from the palace.

"Look at that house so full of light," said the goddess. "I must go there." She traveled down and stepped up to the door, ready to enter and give her blessings to the family that welcomed her so. But in the doorway stood a young woman with a broom, blocking the way.

"You can not come in here, for you left us before," said Shantha.

"Please, my dear," said the goddess. "I am tired and wish to come and rest for a moment. Do be kind."

"Only if you promise to leave your blessing with us forever," said the woman. The goddess agreed at last and entered the house. She glowed goldenlike as she sat, graciously served by Shantha. Lakshmi enjoyed her stay and was true to her word, blessing the family when she went on her way.

From that day on, the hard work of the three was well rewarded and their fortune multiplied. The old king had learned his lesson and now enjoyed the feeling of good, honest work more than the pleasures of gambling. When their riches grew greater and greater, they were able to return to their own kingdom. The young son, with Shantha, began to rule. Their reign was a good one, for they continued to work hard, to live simply, and to share the blessings of the Goddess Lakshmi.

The Wise Merchant

PAKISTAN

Once in Pakistan, there lived a merchant who was both wise and hard-working. He had a son, though, who loved nothing more than playing and lazing around. He never lifted a hand to help out, yet spent rupees as if they were curds flowing through his fingers. And so, as the merchant grew older, he grew very worried.

"My son can not do a good day's work. He does not realize how hard you must work to build and keep wealth. What can I do to teach him?" he wondered. Then, just as he thought of a plan, his son came up to him.

"Father, give me some money to invest in a business," he demanded.

"I shall lend you the money," said the father, "if you can pass this test." He walked to the well in the courtyard, took out a coin, and threw it into the water.

"Until I tell you to stop, you must throw one coin down into the well every day," said the merchant. "When I see that you are ready, I will lend you what you need."

The boy thought this an easy test. Every evening, after doing nothing all day, he took a coin from his mother and threw it into the well. His father watched and then asked her not to help the boy. The next day, when his mother refused to give, the boy went to his married sister's home. He started to throw her money daily into the well.

Soon, the merchant stopped her help, too, and the boy tried his aunt. He used her coins until his father ended that supply. Next the boy took money from his uncle, until his father talked to the uncle as well.

At last the son could find no one to give him money. He grew desperate and decided to work in the nearby town. Since he had no training in a trade, the only job he could find was as a day laborer. He worked very hard all day, carrying heavy loads. At the end of the day he received just one coin. He ran home, holding it tightly.

He walked up to the well and his father joined him. But suddenly, it was very difficult to throw away the money. He felt exhausted; his muscles pained him so after the long day's work. He remembered how hot and tired he had been. Finally, he threw the coin down into the well, very quietly.

The next day, he carried heavy loads again until his muscles cried. And that night, he found it hard to throw his precious earnings into the well. For a week this continued until one night as he stepped up to the well, his father stopped him.

"My son," said the merchant, "tonight, the test is finished. You may keep this coin you truly earned. I believe at last you understand the value of hard work and of money. Now I can trust you with my savings."

The next day, happy children fished most of the coins out of the well. And soon after that, the merchant gave his son a large sum, which he spent wisely in trading.

For many years, the family prospered, since the young man worked well with his father. After the merchant died at last, the son worked harder still, and he never, ever again wasted even the smallest of coins.

Nature and Humans

7

Even a one-half-inch insect has a one-half-inch soul.
—**Japanese proverb**

In Japan, the shift of the season is deeply felt: each time has its own flowers, fruits, and mood. In many Muslim lands, the word *Jannat* (Garden) means Heaven and the image of a fine garden represents paradise on earth. In China, Vietnam, and Korea, the earth itself is special for it holds the bones of the ancestors, and so binds the living to those gone on. India calls the river Ganges especially sacred and pilgrims come from afar to bathe in it.

Asian landscapes are grand indeed: the rich rain forests of Southeast Asia, the desserts of Pakistan and India, the awesome Himalayas, the endless miles of perfect beaches. Legends of these varied lands are widespread and important in Asia.

Animals range from the tiny mousedeer of Southeast Asia to the sturdy Asian elephants found in temples, work camps, and stories. Foxes and rabbits live both in forests and in trickster tales, while tigers, endangered as they are in life, still roar through folk stories. Asians tell of mythical animals—dragons, the phoenix, unicorns—as well as of marriages between animals and humans. Animals are often symbols in stories: the gentle cow of India; the long-lived crane of Japan; the sacred, fierce, or witless tiger in Korea; the twelve animals ruling the calendar years in much of East Asia.

Although there are many vegetarians in Asia, some groups have always hunted animals—and often with respect. Ainu leader Shigeru Kayano remembers his father's words every year as he bowed both to the first salmon of the season and to the Ainu Goddess of Fire: "Today, for the first time this year, I have brought home a salmon. Please rejoice. This salmon is not merely for us humans to eat by ourselves, but for us to eat with the gods and with my children, as tiny as insects. Please watch over me, that I may catch many salmon hereafter."[1]

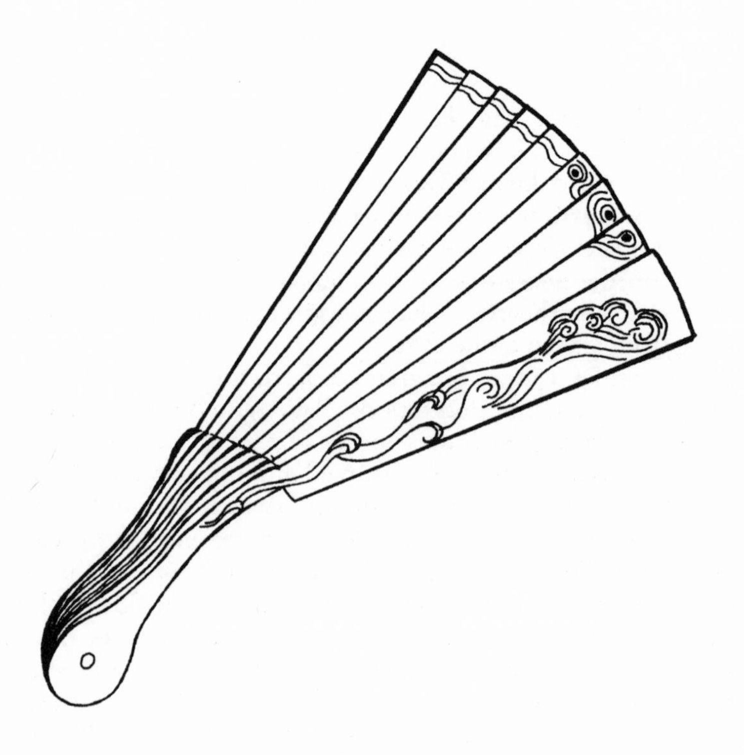

The Scratch

INDIA

Non-violence and compassion toward all living beings are practiced by several Asian faiths. In this short Indian teaching tale, the Goddess Parvati is seen as the Mother of all, the center of a web of life uniting various living forms.

Once on the top of sacred Mount Kailasa, Ganesh, the elephant-headed god, was playing in the garden. Nearby in the house, his mother, the Goddess Parvati, was making supper. Ganesh, feeling bored, picked up a little kitten and played with her quite roughly. She made sad sounds to make him stop, but he didn't listen. He kept bouncing and shaking her. Finally, he tired of this game and dropped the kitten, scratching her face by mistake as he did.

Ganesh then went in to see his mother. But he stopped at the door when he saw fresh blood on her face.

"Mother, who did that to you?" he asked, full of fury. "I will teach them a lesson right now. No one can hurt you. I won't let them."

"But my son, you gave me this scratch," she replied sadly.

"No, I didn't. I would never hurt you," he protested.

"You did not know you were hurting me, my child," she said softly. "But when you just scratched that little kitten, my face was scratched. Whenever you hurt any part of nature, you harm me, and all of nature as well. Be careful, my son."

A Girl, A Horse

JAPAN

According to folklore collector and scholar Koji Inada, the marriage between human and animal is a very important theme in Japanese folk tales. In this story from northern Tohoku, a fine friendship between horse and human helps explain the origin of beautiful silk.

Mukashi, mukashi ...

Once, in the cold north of Japan, a girl was born. On the same night and nearby, a boy colt, too, came into this world. From her earliest days, the girl was kind and caring, loved by all. And that bright white horse, gentle and strong like bamboo, grew with the child.

In those long-ago times, in that faraway land, horses lived with the families they served. Thus one room inside the girl's home belonged to the young horse. To him every night, the girl brought warm food, bidding him eat before she touched her rice. To him every morning, she brought mountain water, rubbing and brushing his hair as he drank.

As soon as his legs were sturdy enough, the girl began to ride on him for hours, as season followed season. When the moon whispered to the mountains in summer, the girl on the horse galloped home through fireflies. When the sun glowed warm on fall rice, the girl on the horse leapt across the pampas grass. And when there was work in the fields of spring, the girl walked beside the horse, helping.

Years passed in such friendly pleasures and the girl was soon of an age to be wed. Yet she showed no interest in marriage to others. She preferred to stay home, to play with her friend, the horse.

"You cannot spend all of your time with that animal. We will find you a husband," said her parents. But the girl simply shook her head and stared at the floor. Young men were brought by the matchmakers, but the girl hid when they came. Finally, one night she faced her parents and said, "I am happy as I am. I do not wish to marry; my life is content. If I must marry, I will marry my best friend, the horse."

Her parents were now most upset. "We must get rid of that animal," decided the mother. "Only then will our child do as we say." So, early the next day, her parents sent the girl alone on an errand to a far village. At twilight, before she returned, the couple led the horse into the mountains and high, high up to a steep cliff. They pulled the horse nearer to the edge, ready to push him far below.

"*Heeeee heeeeehhh,*" cried the horse, calling his friend. All at once, the thunder god beat upon his drum, "*Da-don, Da-don.*" A sudden storm raged and a spear of light appeared. In that instant, the horse disappeared. Pleased that their problem was solved, the couple went home alone.

Late that night, the girl returned, greeted her parents, and rushed to the horse's room.

"*Ahhhhhhh!*" Her scream tore through the house as she cried, "Where is he? What have you done?"

"He ran away to the mountains," they lied.

"No, he would never leave me. I'll find him," she shouted and raced off, calling his name again and again.

"Dear friend, come back, come home," she begged for hours and hours, pushing aside the dark. Her parents followed her into that stormy night, climbing higher and higher in the mountains. The old couple, so afraid for their child, soon lost sight of her and wandered hopelessly until, all at once, they saw her for the last time.

Standing still on a cliff, her arms stretched out, her mouth open in a cry, she was circled by a sudden brilliance from the sky. Then blackness returned with a last roar of thunder. After that came only silence for she, too, had vanished into that raging night.

The couple groped on in the dark, calling her name again and again. Their cries wove through the shadows, fearful and pleading. Yet only a soft rain sounded in reply. Hours later, the sun crept out; the mountain smiled again. And the tired couple, overwhelmed by their loss, suddenly looked down. There, on a mossy rock, they found two small worms huddled close together.

Gently, they picked up the worms. For somehow the couple knew that their daughter and her best friend now lived in these little creatures. At home, they nurtured the worms, feeding them from a mulberry tree in the yard. The mother spoke kindly, singing to them her daughter's favorite lullabies. In a few days, the plumb worms started to spin and spin and spin. Soft white cocoons soon covered the two.

Tenderly, the father placed them under the thatch roof, watching them daily. One morning, the cocoons stood deserted and the reds of dawn swirled round two lovely white moths. Like pieces of lace, they danced round the lonely couple, then joyfully circled the house.

After several days of play, the moths dipped their wings in a final good-by and flew off together toward the mountains. With silent faces, the couple stared at the sky for a long time. Then they saw, near their door, several tiny, perfect eggs left by the moths. They gathered the eggs and placed them carefully in a box, along with mulberry leaves. Soon the eggs hatched into little silkworms.

Somehow, as if told by their daughter, the parents knew what to do and they helped those first silkworms to make long, fine silk thread. Months and years passed. And although the parents often longed for their child, her gift of silk helped them to live comfortably until death closed their eyes.

People share this story still today in the north of Japan. They say that silk, with its delicate strength, came from this friendship, strong and tender. And even now, those who tell this tale know that the finest silk floss is gathered only when lightning and thunder storm in the mountains, as they once did on that long-ago night.

The Right Site

KOREA

The art of placing buildings and burial sites in harmony with natural surroundings is an important tradition for many Asian people. Indeed, scholar Hong-Key Yoon concludes that "the impact of geomancy on Korean culture has been both deep and extensive; the use of land can hardly be understood apart from it."[2]

Once in Korea, a young woman from a rich home was married to a man from a noble but impoverished family. She was a model daughter-in-law, taking very good care of her husband and his elder parents, never complaining, and always working hard.

But when her father-in-law died after some time, she was much worried. For in Korea it is most important to be buried well, to have one's grave in an auspicious place so that future generations will be blessed. But it is hard to know all the signs of a good site, and her husband's family was too poor to hire someone to help them.

Now at this same time, there was another death in her own family. Her father died and his family wanted, of course, to bury him in the best site. Since there was much money in that family, they hired a geomancer, someone who knew the land and its secrets, to find the correct place.

When the young bride was visiting her childhood home, she happened to hear the geomancer's words describing a good site he had found. "We must check in the morning, after tonight's rain. If it is dry tomorrow, then it will bring great fortune to the family as a gravesite. However, if it is wet, then ill luck and tragedy will shadow your blood."

The clever young woman crept out of her house late that night, carrying a large jar of water. She found the gravesite and saw that it was still dry. Knowing it to be a very good spot, she happily poured water all over the ground, then returned home. The next day, she again saw the geomancer come in, this time with a most mournful face.

"I am afraid that the site is of no use," he told her mother. "This morning it was full of water. I will go now to seek another place of better fortune." After he left, the young woman went to her mother, wearing a very sad expression.

"Forgive me, mother, but I heard the words of that man. I know that you have a worthless gravesite. Might I beg you to give it to my husband's family since it is of no use to you. As you know, they are very poor and can not afford the help of a geomancer. They will be much pleased with me if I give them this site in your name." The mother agreed and her daughter hurried home with her good news.

Her father-in-law's body was buried there, and from that day on the poor family's fortunes increased. Money came to stay in their home and illustrious sons were born, all because the proper gravesite had been found.

The Children

LAOS

"How-and-why" tales are popular in Asia, and many of them describe the origins of various plants and animals. Often such stories offer warnings that nourish important cultural values.

Once in Laos, a large family lived in happiness for many years. And then a drought covered the land, causing great pain. Year after year of hardship reduced the family to terrible poverty. Every day, the parents went into the woods seeking food while their ten children scoured the riverbeds.

One day, the children found twelve small crabs. Joyfully they ran home and the eldest sister cooked them into a soup. It smelled so good that the children couldn't wait to eat. They each sipped the soup, ate one crab, and saved the two last crabs for their parents. But the youngest boy's stomach felt so empty that he couldn't stop crying. He begged and begged for just one more crab. Finally, his sister gave him what was left, and the children went to bed. Much later, the hungry parents returned to delicious smells and empty shells.

"Husband," said the wife, "our children did not care enough to save us food, even knowing how weak we are. It is difficult to feed them; it is sorrowful to watch them starve. Let us take them tomorrow into the woods and leave them. They may be able to survive there." Her husband sadly agreed and at last they slept, stomachs aching. But the oldest girl had heard their plan and she soon crawled outside to gather and hide many white pebbles.

The next morning, the children went to the woods eagerly with their parents. When they came to the quiet heart of the forest, the parents said, "Children, rest here for a moment while we go pick some fruits." The children waited, enjoying the forest at first. But as the sounds in the woods grew louder and the shadows grew larger, they were afraid.

"It's all right," said the eldest calmly. "This trail of white pebbles will lead us home." Smiling once again, the children quickly found their way back.

At first, the parents were glad to see them. Yet when after a week nothing had changed, the two whispered a plan that the eldest girl did not hear. And so, once again, the children found themselves alone in the forest, but this time without a trail. They spent night after fearsome night lost and confused. Then slowly, as day followed day, the children began to like the forest. They became friends with the animals; they learned which berries and forest fruits to eat.

Several years passed, and rains came at last. The parents flourished and soon had money enough for a big family again. So one day, they made the children's favorite foods and went seeking them. For many days they searched through the forest, but there was no sign of the young ones. At last, heartbroken, they were ready to return when the mother spied ten faces in a tree, watching her. She recognized her children, although they had changed greatly. With a smile she called to them.

"Children, please forgive us and return home. We miss you so. Come quickly, I have your favorite rice and fish here. And at home now we have more food for you."

At first there was no answer in the silent forest; then a voice cried out, "Mother, you left us here alone. Now the forest is our home. Our arms have become long from swinging on trees; our hair covers us to keep us warm; our teeth are too sharp for your soft rice. We belong here, and we can't return. Go back to your home. It is no longer ours."

With a swish of leaves, the ten monkeys turned and jumped away into the forest, swinging gracefully from tree to tree. The parents watched as they went farther and farther away, and in a few moments there was no sign of them. The couple stood without moving until the silence of the forest grew too sad. Then, still holding their children's favorite foods, the two returned sorrowfully to a quiet, empty home.

8 Faith and Belief

The best richness is the richness of the soul.
—**sayings of Prophet Muhammad**

Faith remains a part not just of storytelling, but of life in much of Asia. Asian religions and philosophies form a rich mosaic. Buddhism is followed in most of East and Southeast Asia; Islam is dominant in parts of the region's south and southeast. In Vietnam, Korea, China, Taiwan, and Singapore, various combinations of Buddhist, Confucian, and Daoist philosophy have flourished over the years. Hinduism, important historically in parts of Southeast Asia, is strong today in India and Nepal. Christianity also is followed in Asia, especially in the Philippines (almost 85 percent Christian) and in Korea.

In Korea, Shamanism provides a foundation for much thought, just as Shintoism is a part of life to many in Japan. Indigenous peoples throughout Asia often have great respect for nature's powers, among other beliefs.

Many of these faiths offer solace, advice, and help with life's journeys and turning points. Many of them are passed on through stories, sayings, ballads, and songs. Storytellers often have made the gods and saints seem more accessible, more like men and women, so that humans can relate to them. Buddhist and Jain storytellers of old frequently carried pictures of hell as they told their tales. And countless Asian grandparents have for centuries told tales of their beliefs to eager young listeners.

God in All

INDIA

Once a monk went about his begging rounds and stood before a rich man's house just as the door opened. Then suddenly, the wealthy owner pushed a servant out and began to beat him.

"Stop, please, sir," said the monk. "He is a man like yourself." However, these kind words only made the rich man angrier. He stopped beating his servant and attacked the monk. With both fists flying, he punched the monk and hit him until he fell to the ground, hardly moving. Then the rich man stomped back into his house and locked the door.

Sometime later, several other monks walked by and recognized the poor monk. With great care, they carried him back to their temple. Very gently, they put a wet cloth on his forehead and when he slowly opened his eyes, they called for milk. One of the monk's good friends slowly spooned it into the patient's mouth. To make sure that the monk was not badly injured, his friend bent down and softly asked, "Brother, do you know who is giving you milk?"

The monk replied in a weak voice, "The one who beat me is now giving me milk."

A Final Lesson

CHINA

In parts of East Asia, both Daoist and Confucian thought have been important influences. Confucianism promoted order, filial piety, and a hierarchy both within society and within the family. Daoism spoke of a natural harmony, maintained through humility, moderation, and the flexible nature illustrated in the next story.

Once a great philosopher in China grew ill and his disciples gathered to help. One of them was the famous Laozi who later wrote the wise book, *Daode Jing.* He begged his teacher for some final advice.

"Get out of your carriage when you near your birthplace," said the teacher. "Why so?"

"Because I should never forget my homeland," replied Laozi.

His teacher nodded, then opened his mouth wide. After he closed it he said, "I still have my tongue. But are my teeth there?"

"They are all gone, sir," replied Laozi.

"And why is that?"

"Is it because your tongue is soft and can be moved, while your teeth are all gone because they were too hard?"

"You are right, dear student. I have nothing left to teach you."

A Good Beating

TIBET

In Buddhist practice, people often repeat the vow "I take refuge in the Buddha, the Dharma, the Sangha. I take refuge in the Triple Gem." The words show a belief in the Buddha, in his teachings (the Dharma), and in the community of monks (the Sangha). Another phrase regularly repeated by Tibetan Buddhists is "Om Mani Padme Hung," *"Hail to the jewel in the lotus," a mantra both simple and profound.*

Once in Tibet there dwelt a kind old monk who lived in a clean and simple cave. Every day he said his prayers, meditated for long hours, and often repeated, "Om Mani Padme Hung." He lived a very simple life and had only one valuable possession—a set of silver bowls in which he offered clean water daily to the deities.

Near the monk, in a small village, lived a thief ever eager for wealth. One day, he saw the old man pouring water into his fine bowls. From then on, the thief began to watch the old man, planning how to steal the silver bowls.

At last one night he crept up to the cave. He heard the old man saying his various prayers, and then there was silence. Seeing only a small light, the thief felt sure that the man was asleep. Quietly he crawled into the cave, closer and closer to the silver bowls. He glanced at the old man. He was sitting, but his eyes were closed.

"Old fool," thought the thief. "He fell asleep while trying to pray." Quickly, he reached out to take the bowls when suddenly something hit his arm.

"I take refuge in the Buddha, the Dharma, the Sangha. I take refuge in the Triple Gem," said the old monk loudly, hitting the thief with a prayer book. For the monk had been meditating, not sleeping, and thus he saw the thief approach. Now the old man was not greedy, and didn't care for possessions. Yet he knew that the thief would be in greater trouble if he continued to steal. So the monk hit the man, while saying those words, to help save him.

Much surprised and holding his aching arm, the thief fled from the cave. He ran toward his home when all of a sudden great and terrible shapes began to form around him. He was soon surrounded by horrible spirits and monsters. Closer and closer they came in the dark, making frightful groans and moans. As he shivered in terror, he remembered the words of the monk. He called them out in a weak voice, "I take refuge in the Buddha, the Dharma, the Sangha. I take refuge in the Triple Gem."

The shapes suddenly weakened. Some disappeared, others grew dim. Bolder now, he repeated, "I take refuge in the Buddha, the Dharma, the Sangha. I take refuge in the Triple Gem." More of them fled. He said the words one last time to find all the creatures gone.

From that day on, the thief was a changed man. He began to repeat those words often. Then he started to go to the old monk, to learn other prayers, to be taught more about his faith. The thief was a quick pupil and when the old man died, the former thief moved into his cave. Soon he had pupils of his own and he led them to the pure light of Buddhism. And thus he lived a long and rich life in that simple cave, well proving the power of faith and prayer delivered with the right touch.

Salmaan al-Faarsi

Pakistan

Tales in Muslim cultures often share the lives of the Prophet Muhammad, of his companions, or of his followers. The story of Salmaan al-Faarsi is one such inspiring and fascinating tale. It is the grand adventure of a boy born into a rich Persian family who ran off to study Christianity, was sold as a slave, met and followed the Prophet Muhammad, then finished his days as a respected governor. Here are two small anecdotes from his simple lifestyle of faith and modesty.

Once when Salmaan was governor of Al-Madaa'in, he was walking down the street in the plain, older clothes he usually wore. A stranger in the city saw him and thought him a poor man, a laborer.

"Come carry this for me and you'll get a bit of bread," said the man, pointing to a bag that Salmaan quietly picked up. As they walked down the street, people bowed to Salmaan in respect while the stranger watched in growing confusion. Then someone greeted Salmaan politely by his official title.

"I beg your forgiveness, sir," said the now frightened stranger. "Do give me back my bag. I made a terrible mistake and insulted you greatly. Please don't punish me." But Salmaan only shook his head gently and insisted upon carrying the bag to the newcomer's door. Then, with a smile, he left, wishing the man well.

Years later, Salmaan became weak and knew he would soon die. A friend came to visit him on his deathbed. All of a sudden, Salmaan al-Faarsi began to cry.

"Why are you crying, friend?" asked the visitor.

"I am not weeping for fear of death or from sadness at leaving this world," he replied. "I'm crying because the Prophet instructed us to live in this world as travelers, and here I own too many pieces of property."

His friend knew that Salmaan was a generous man, giving his salary away in charity while dressing and eating in great simplicity. So he looked around to see what property seemed so much. He saw little of anything in the room.

"What pieces of property do you mean?" he asked. And Salmaan al-Faarsi pointed to two bowls—one for eating, one for washing. That was all that he had. Yet that was the property that made him weep in shame.

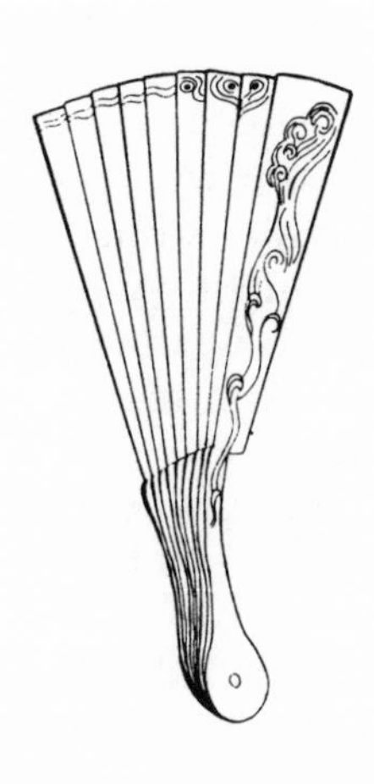

Kirihataji

JAPAN

One of the "Five Pillars of Islam" for Asian Muslims is the Hajj, a pilgrimage to the holy city of Makkah. It is a most special event, to be saved for over a lifetime. Those who have gone are welcomed home with celebration and treated with great respect. Elsewhere in Asia, pilgrims of different faiths go on pilgrimages as well, on foot, in car, by bus. One of the most famous pilgrimages in Japan is to each of the eighty-eight temples of the great saint and sage Kobo Daishi, on the island of Shikoku. There are stories all along the pilgrim trail ...

Once Kobo Daishi came to a quiet mountainside. There he found a lovely girl who sat weaving in a small hut. She very kindly provided food for him while he prayed and meditated for seven days on the mountain. When he was ready to leave, he asked for a little cloth to wrap round his legs. At once she cut him lovely pieces to warm his legs as well as a fine large piece to make a new coat.

Kobo Daishi was very curious now to know how such a warm-hearted young girl came to live in such an isolated way. She told him her story.

"My mother was a court lady until my father joined with others to overthrow the emperor. The plan was discovered and he was exiled. At that time, my mother was pregnant and much afraid that if she had a boy, he would be killed. Daily she went to Kiyomizu Temple in Kyoto to pray for a girl. Kannon, the merciful, granted her wish and I was born. After several years, Kannon appeared in a dream telling my mother to flee. The two of us came here and hid. When my mother later grew ill, she told me the story and begged me to worship Kannon faithfully. Since her death, I have followed her request with great care."

Much impressed with her faith, Kobo Daishi began to

carve a statue of Kannon for the girl. He followed the strict rules of bowing three times before each cut of the wood. At last a wondrous statue was carved. The girl then wished to become a nun. She cut her hair and took her vows before Kobo Daishi. At that moment, a violet cloud came from the heavens and wondrous music was heard. The nun immediately attained Buddhahood and turned into a statue of Kannon.

Kobo Daishi carefully took the two statues and founded a temple on the mountain, putting them in a place of honor. The name came from its beginnings: *kiri* means cut, *hata* means cloth, and *ji* indicates a temple; thus the temple is Kirihataji.

Valli and Kande Yaka

Sri Lanka

This old love story involving a girl and a god comes courtesy of American researcher Patrick Harrigan, who remarks: "The tale remains etched in the imaginations of countless Sri Lankans and South Indians, most of whom first heard it recited by their mothers, grandmothers, or grandfathers. Valli's story shares a timeless theme of the unseen and unrecognized descent of the Spirit that carries away and weds the yearning human soul."

In the Indian Ocean not far from India lies a teardrop-shaped jewel of a tropical island called Lanka. Many thousands of years ago—nobody knows for certain when—Stone Age people of ancient India walked to Lanka across a narrow bridge of land, called Adam's Bridge, and populated this island of paradise. Their descendants today call themselves *Wanniya-laeto* or "inhabitants of the forest." But most Sri Lankans call them *Vaddas*, meaning hunters.

Vaddas believed that the spirit of a great hunter lived upon a remote mountain peak within sight of the Indian Ocean. Kande Yaka, the Great Mountain-Spirit and Hunter-God, was the Vadda people's greatest friend and guardian spirit, then even as he still is today. No successful hunt began without Vadda hunters first dancing themselves into a trance-frenzy in which Kande Yaka spoke through them, telling them where to hunt and how to survive happily. But the Vadda people also knew that Kande Yaka was easily angered, so all regarded him with a mixture of love, respect, and fear.

Now Vaddas are a people who are accustomed to marvelous occurrences. So when Nambi, the chief of the Kataragama Vaddas, and his wife one day discovered a baby girl in the jungle, they were overjoyed because they had been praying for a daughter. Yet nobody considered it a miracle. They called her Valli, meaning "Sweet Potato," because they found her in a patch of yam or valli creepers. Some say her real mother was a red deer, so perhaps Valli also had reddish hair and wide innocent eyes of a doe. Others say that since Nambi was the Vaddas' chief, therefore Valli was a Vadda princess. But all agree that Valli was the sweetest child anyone had ever seen, and everyone adored her.

Valli's girlfriends loved her too, but they couldn't help but tease her about the peculiar promise she had made. Valli was twelve years old and her girlfriends were always talking about brave, handsome Vadda boys who were already hunters themselves. But Valli had vowed to herself—and to Kande Yaka—that she would only accept Kande Yaka and no one else as her life companion. All the other Vadda girls laughed and made fun of Valli for vowing to marry a god whom no one had seen.

But Kande Yaka had been watching all his Vadda people, including Valli, with great interest all this time. The hunter-god of the mountain was as old as the mountain itself. But as a spirit he was also young, just like Valli. Before long, the ever-youthful Kande Yaka felt so attracted to Valli that he decided to come down from his mountain and meet her.

At the time, Valli's family had cleared a small patch in the jungle near Kataragama Peak and they were growing millet there. But someone had to stand guard against parrots and other birds that came to eat the millet. Valli, who grew up in the jungle, was not afraid of being alone, so her father sent her to guard the field while he and his sons went hunting with bow and arrows. Day and night Valli's sweet voice could be heard as she sang to the birds and animals, warning them to keep away and twirling a sling that she used to fling stones if they ignored her and tried to eat the tender millet.

Kande Yaka could see that this was his chance to meet Valli alone face-to-face. So just like you or I would put on a fresh change of clothes, Kande Yaka put on the human form of a handsome young hunter. He figured this would be the best way to impress her. Pretending to be tracking a deer, he strolled out of the forest and into the millet field. Of course, Valli could not recognize the handsome stranger.

"Hey, get out of here fast and don't come back!" she yelled, adding, "Who do you think you are?" Poor Kande Yaka was just about to apologize and retreat back into the forest when suddenly there was the sound of drums—Nambi and his hunters were bringing Valli some mangoes and honey to eat.

The moment Valli looked away, Kande Yaka turned himself into a tree. As soon as the hunters left, the god reappeared in human form and confessed his love for her. Valli was shocked and angry, and told the stranger to beware or her brothers would come back and go wild if they saw him there alone with her.

Just at that moment there was the sound of footsteps and they knew that Valli's family was coming back. In the blink of an eye, Kande Yaka changed himself into an old man with long gray beard bent over with age. Valli's family paid their respects to the kind old man and suggested that Valli would be good company for the old man as long as he stayed.

As soon as the hunting party left, the old man told Valli he was hungry, so she gave him some millet flour mixed with honey. This only made him thirsty, so she took him to a stream and gave him water to drink. Then he told her, "Now that you have satisfied my hunger and thirst, do satisfy my love for you."

This was too much for Valli, so she gave the strange old man a piece of her mind and was about to start back to the clearing. Kande Yaka mentally asked his brother the elephant-god Ganesh for assistance. Instantly from out of the jungle behind Valli came Ganesh in the form of a wild trumpeting elephant. Valli got the fright of her life, rushed back into the arms of the old man and begged him to save her. "I'll save you, but on one condition," he said. "You must marry me."

There was no time to argue, so Valli agreed. No sooner did Valli agree to the stranger's condition than he revealed himself as Kande Yaka, seated on a peacock and surrounded by dazzling light. Valli was thrilled to see that it was her beloved god and after that they were never apart.

Never, except that soon the time of harvesting the millet approached, and her family called Valli back to their tribal hamlet. Kande Yaka was awfully upset when he came to the clearing and could not find Valli. So late at night he slipped into the hamlet and together they ran away.

When Vadda chief Nambi woke up in the morning, he realized that Valli had run away with the old man and he was furious. He organized a search party and set out to get revenge. When they found them, they released a volley of arrows, but instead of killing the mysterious old man, the Vaddas all fell dead instead.

Valli was stricken with grief to see her relatives dead. Seeing her sorrow, Kande Yaka told her to revive them, which she did simply by touching them. The Vaddas at once realized that Valli's friend was the great god of the mountain himself, and they all fell down to worship him.

Valli's parents gave their consent for the couple to be married and the whole village rejoiced. Since that time long ago, Valli and Kande Yaka have never left Kataragama and have never died, either. And they still have fun like other children, playing hide-and-seek with each other and with their devotees, who come in search of them from all over the island and even from far, far away. And if you don't believe it, you can go to Kataragama and find out for yourself.

9

Fantasy and the Supernatural

The spirits hover but three feet above your head.
—Chinese proverb

In Asia, as elsewhere, tales of ghosts, spirits, and strange worlds are much enjoyed. In Japan, the *rakugo* story-teller will often include ghost tales in his summer perfomances to cool people off with a few chills. In India, wandering tellers share many ballads about humans, usually women or low caste people, who are killed most unjustly and thus come back as vengeful spirits.

Various supernatural beings show up in the region's tales: *jinn* are popular in Muslim stories as magical creatures that can both help and hinder, while in Indian tales, *rakshasa* are demons to avoid. Across East Asia, foxes, tigers, and badgers often change shapes to make trouble or to find love, while in parts of the Asian Pacific Rim, tales can include a Water Kingdom far below.

Zhuang Brocade

CHINA

Long ago in China, there was a woman who could weave magic. She wove cloth so lifelike you would swear it was real. If she wove a peach, you could feel its juice drip down your chin. If she wove incense, you could smell the sharp smoke. If she wove the breeze, it stroked your skin. Since her cloth was so wondrous, she sold it with ease and thus could support her three sons.

One day she was in a small shop, exchanging cloth for rice. Suddenly she looked up and saw a new painting on the wall. It was of a land far away and quite magical. A cool marble pavilion stood in the shadow of a cliff. Bamboo swayed proudly, pines beckoned, and deer grazed near a pond full of shining carp. Looking at it gave her such peace that she knew she must have the painting.

"Would you trade that picture for more of my cloth?" she asked the merchant hopefully. Well pleased, he agreed at once and the woman soon started home, clutching the painting. She stopped often on the way, simply to gaze at its quiet beauty.

After she returned home, she showed the painting to her eldest son and asked, "Wouldn't you love to live in this land?"

"Foolish woman," he said. "You can't live in a painting."

She turned to her second son, saying, "How about you? You would like to live here, no?"

"Get back to work, mother," he replied with a laugh, "and stop this nonsense."

Sadly, the mother went to her youngest son and softly asked, "My son, would you like to live near this pond?"

The boy looked at his mother, then at the painting, before he spoke.

"Mother," he said gently, "you can't live in a picture, that is true. But you weave such marvelous cloth. Why don't you weave this painting, and then when we look at it, we will feel as if we live right in it."

"Ah, yes, I will. I must," she said eagerly. Quickly, she gathered her finest silk thread and set up her loom. She began to work long, long hours weaving and weaving.

Her three sons now had to chop wood steadily to support the family. So when a year had passed and she was still not done, the two older boys were much annoyed.

"Mother," they cried, "you must give up this useless idea and get back to your real work." But her youngest son said at once, "No, mother must finish. I will chop enough for our needs."

Thus the young boy had to chop all day and into the dark, while his mother worked equally hard. She began to burn pine needles to light the night. When another year had almost passed, her eyes one day pained so much that great tears fell upon her work. But she did not push them away. Instead, she wove them right into the cloth and they became a strong, flowing river running through the magical land.

On and on she worked and now three years were almost over. Her fingers ached, her eyes burned. One night as she worked, great drops of blood fell from her eyes, right upon the cloth. But again, she did not push the blood aside. Rather, she wove it into the cloth and the blood turned into the brightest red flowers and a brilliant sun.

Then at last, the cloth was finished. With trembling fingers, she removed it from the loom and showed it to her sons. They were amazed at what she had done.

"Mother, it is truly beautiful," they agreed. "You have woven a miracle."

Well pleased, the mother took the cloth outside, so that the heavens themselves could see. She laid the cloth gently down on the ground, but suddenly a breeze came and carried it away.

"*Come back!*" she cried running after it. "*Come back* ..." But it was gone and she collapsed upon the ground. She cried out to her sons, begging them to find her cloth. The eldest son soon started off in search of it. He journeyed for almost a month, resting often, sleeping late. Finally, he came to a mountain and saw a stone house, a stone horse, stone berries, and a woman made of stories, not stone.

"Old woman, have you seen my mother's fine cloth?" he called out.

"Oh yes," she said. "The fairies from Sun Mountain have taken it as a model for their needlework. You can try to get it back, but it will be very hard. First, you must take a rock and break off your two front teeth. Then place them in my horse's mouth and mount him. He will eat my stone berries, then take you over Flame Mountain, where the fire will burn you. But you must not cry out, not even a whisper, or you will die.

"If you make it through the fire, you will come to the Sea of Ice, where great frozen blocks will crash all round you. If you so much as shudder, you will be crushed. If by some chance you make it through, you will come to Sun Mountain. If you reach the top, perhaps the fairies will give you the cloth. Or perhaps they will make you disappear forever!"

The son felt his two front teeth and started to shiver.

"I knew you couldn't do it," said the women. She reached down and offered him a small box. "Here, take this bit of gold and be gone."

Eagerly he snatched it and ran away. But, being a greedy soul, he decided to go live in the city, alone, and to keep the gold all for himself.

When he did not return, the second son was sent. He met the same woman, heard the same words, and took the gold as well. Back in the mother's poor house, after long months of waiting, she was now as thin as a twig, her eyes almost blind from tears.

"My son, you must go and hurry, please," she begged. Her youngest son set off, running day and night until he came to the mountain. He listened to the woman and, as she reached down for gold, picked up a rock and knocked out his teeth. Quickly he pushed them into the stone horse, who ate the berries, and at once the two flew over Flame Mountain.

Wild fingers of fire licked all about him, but his love helped him stay still. Next they came to the Sea of Ice. It was so cold he longed to scream and scream, but then, as in a dream, he felt a warm breeze and saw Sun Mountain.

Up a cloud ladder he climbed to the top. There he saw a fine jade pavilion, with curtains of crystal, and inside, lovely ladies wearing silks rich with dragons and unicorns. In the midst of a grand hall, he saw his mother's cloth, proudly displayed upon a golden stand. All the fairies were trying to copy it, so when he reached out to take it, they cried, "No, please, we are almost finished. Give us just one more night."

The kindhearted boy agreed and they served him lichee nuts and peach blossom wine. Soon he slept, while a lovely girl in bright red finished her cloth. She took it up to the mother's and compared the two. Then her face grew sad. For her river was not as full of life, her flowers seemed so pale, her sun had no strength. So all of a sudden, she took some red thread, stitched herself into the cloth, and disappeared.

Just then, the boy awoke, snatched the cloth, and returned down the mountain. He made it through the Sea of Ice, over Flame Mountain, and back to the old woman.

"Hurry," she said, "your mother is almost dead." She gave him his teeth and special shoes to make him fly. He was home in seconds and rushed to his mother.

"Here is the cloth," he said softly and put it on her chest. The woman could hardly see, but she held it up slowly and its brilliance pierced through the gloom of the hut. She gazed now on what she had made, on the work of many years, and she felt a great peace.

Carefully, she took it outside again, to share with the heavens. She placed it on the ground and again a breeze came. But this was a kind breeze. It did not take her weaving; it simply stretched the cloth—to the north, the south, the east, the west. And as the cloth grew and grew, suddenly the family's hut disappeared and the weeds of their old garden vanished. In their place stood a marble pavilion, a fine cliff of bamboo and pine, some deer, a pond, and a lovely lady in red.

From that day on, the mother, her son, and the fairy from Sun Mountain lived in great joy. Then one quiet fall afternoon, two tired, ragclad men stumbled up to the gate and peered inside. They heard laughter and recognized voices, but did not enter because of their shame. Thus our story ends as those two walk sadly down the road, and that brilliant red sun slowly sets in the West.

Three Charms

JAPAN

This is a favorite of many Japanese tellers, and I think you'll see why. Yamanbas, besides being fierce, can change their shapes to trick humans. But like other strange creatures in Japanese tales, they also can be beaten by sharp wits and a clever tongue.

Mukashi, mukashi ... Long ago in Japan, a boy lived with a kind monk in a mountainside temple. One fall day, when the hills were ablaze with colors, he thought of the mountain chestnuts ripe and ready.

"Can I please go pick some chestnuts for us?" he asked the monk.

"No, no," he replied. "The yamanba might get you."

"I'm not afraid of any old monster," said the boy.

The monk smiled and shook his head. "She would trick you, little one. Change her shape and eat you up."

"First I would beat her up," bragged the boy.

"I don't think so," replied the monk. But the boy kept on begging and pleading until at last the monk gave in.

"All right, you may go," he said. "But take these three charms for protection." And he handed the student three slips of paper with special writing.

Happily, the boy walked up the path, *su-ta, su-ta,* as maples glowed fiery red and persimmons bloomed ripe orange. Soon, he picked and picked and picked many chestnuts. But when his basket was full, he suddenly noticed that it was very dark, and he was far from home. Shivering a little, the boy looked around and realized that he was lost.

"Shall I return through the shadows?" he wondered, "or find shelter for the night nearby?" Just then, he saw lights glowing up ahead, *pi-ka, pi-ka.* On he walked to a little cottage and knocked, *ton, ton, ton, ton.*

"Ah, do come in," invited the kind-looking older woman who opened the door. The boy asked shyly for a night's stay and she gladly agreed. After a simple meal of rice, beans, and pickle, she spread his *futon* (mat) near the firepit and went to sleep behind a *shoji* paper screen.

The rain fell, *po-ta, po-ta,* as the boy tried to sleep. It was a peaceful sound and he soon snored. Yet when he awoke a little later, the rain seemed to whisper instead "*Abu-nai, abu-nai,* danger, danger."

"I wonder if that nice lady is in trouble," thought the boy. "I must go check." So he crept up to the paper screen, wet his finger, poked a hole through, and peeked in. There he saw ...

A yamanba! A huge, frightful yamanba. Her eyes glowed greedily, *gi-ra, gi-ra.* Her huge red tongue bounced up and down. He turned to run, but she saw him.

"*I'm glad you finally woke up,*" she roared. "*I'm hungry.*"

"Oh, and what would you like to eat?" he whispered.

"*You!*"

"No, you wouldn't."

"*Yes, I would! I love tasty little boys!*"

"But you wouldn't like to eat me now."

"*Why not?*"

"Because ... because ... because I have to go to the bathroom."

"Ugh, you're right," she said. "You wouldn't taste good. You'll have to go to the bathroom first, but I don't want you to run away." She thought for a moment, then tied one end of her *obi* (belt) around his waist and held tightly to the other end as she sent him outside.

"*Hurry up and come back,*" she yelled. The boy walked in the dark to the outhouse. There, he carefully removed the obi, tied it around a post, and slipped one of the charms onto the post.

"Answer in my voice," he said and fled. Meanwhile, back inside, the yamanba waited and waited.

"That boy sure takes a long time," she thought. She tugged the obi and could still feel him there. "*Are you done?*" she cried.

And the boy's voice replied, "I'm coming." So she waited some more.

"What is the problem?" she murmured. She tugged again, he was still there.

"*Hurry up!*" she bellowed. And a voice called out, "Wait. Wait."

After a few more minutes, she called, "You must be finished by now!" But the voice only replied, "Wait, wait."

Hungry and impatient, she pulled angrily on the belt and suddenly the whole outhouse collapsed. She ran out, discovered the trick, and raced off with a cry of rage.

Terrifed, the boy ran as fast as he could, *ba-ta, ba-ta, ba-ta, ba-ta.* Too soon, he heard her crashing close behind him, *fuu-fuu, fuu-fuu.* He threw another charm over his shoulder and cried, "*Make a river!*"

Luckily, a wide river appeared right in front of the yamanba. Unluckily, she could swim. Through the water she hurried, *bacha, bacha,* then started chasing him again, *fuu-fuu, fuu-fuu.*

Looking back, the boy saw her dripping, and ripping up trees. He took out his last charm and threw it behind him, calling, "*Make a mountain!*"

At once, a mountain loomed up, almost knocking the yamanba down. She scrambled over it, gnashing her ugly teeth. On and on raced the boy, back towards the temple and safety. Finally he reached the temple door and knocked desperately, calling, "*Ta-su-ke-te! Help! Help!*"

"Who is it?" asked the monk, although he knew full well.

"It's me! Help!" begged the boy. "The yamanba is after me."

"The yamanba you can beat up?" teased the monk.

"Yes, that one," cried the boy while the monk slowly opened the door. He hid the boy, then sat down peacefully just as the yamanba crashed against the door.

"*AHHHH!*" With a great roar, the yamanba stomped into the room, *Do-shin, Do-shin.*

"*I want that boy! Where did you hide him?*" she bellowed.

"Well, a boy does live here, but he's up on the mountain now," said the monk.

"*No, he's not! I chased him here. Where is he? Show me or I'll eat you up!*"

"Wait, wait, my friend. You do look hungry. Please have some rice cakes as an appetizer," offered the monk. "Then I'll help you find that silly boy." The rice cakes smelled quite nice, so the yamanba sat down and ate about fifty. Wiping her horrible mouth, she started to stand.

"One moment, please," said the monk. "I have heard that you can change yourself into anything at all. Is that true?"

"Yes. Anything I wish," bragged the yamanba.

"What a splendid talent," sighed the monk. "Could you show me how big you can become?"

With a wicked laugh, the yamanba began to grow. Bigger and bigger and bigger she grew until she filled the room and her head pushed against the roof.

"Well done," praised the monk. "And how small can you become? Could you ever be as small as a bean?"

Smiling fiercely, the yamanba twirled her huge body round. Smaller and smaller and smaller she shrank until she was as tiny as a soybean.

"Excellent," said the monk with a chuckle. Then he took his chopsticks, picked her up, chewed her well, and swallowed her down. And that was the end of that yamanba. So they say.

"*Go-chi-so-sa-ma deshita.*" Truly delicious!

The Woodcutter and the Bird

KOREA

This poignant story weaves together several themes found in Korean tales: kindness, gratitude, sacrifice. The large, traditional temple bell pictured here has a heavy log suspended next to it that is pulled back and released to strike on the outside.

Long, long ago, a Korean woodcutter wandered into a forest unknown and strange. As he tried to find his way out, he suddenly heard the cry of a bird, a call full of terror and fright.

The kind woodcutter ran toward the sound and found a mother pheasant trying desperately to scare away a large white snake. The snake was slithering up a tree, moving steadily toward a nest of baby birds. Again and again, the mother pheasant attacked the snake, trying to drive her off. But the snake was not stopped by a mere bird. She just slid closer and closer to the nest.

"*Stop!*" shouted the woodcutter, waving a stick. The snake did not even pause.

"*Go away!*" he cried. Yet the snake kept climbing and was soon next to the birds. She pulled back, preparing to strike. But suddenly the man hit the snake hard on its head and she fell dead to the ground.

With a joyful cry, the mother bird stroked and soothed her young. Then she flew to the woodcutter's shoulder and rested upon it for a moment, as if to give thanks. The woodcutter smiled, pleased that he could help. After a while, he walked on and the day passed. Then the week, the month passed, too, and soon, several years had gone by.

One night, much later, he found himself again in that unknown part of the woods. It was dark and he was lost. He searched round for a place to shelter and finally found a warm light coming from a nearby hut.

He knocked shyly and a woman whiter than the moon opened the door, greeting him softly, "*Ann-yong ha-se-yo.*"

"Excuse me," he begged, "but I am lost and need rest. Might I stay the night in a corner of your home?"

"Please come in," she invited. He sat down and she served him *kimchee* pickle and rice on a low table. As he ate, he marveled at her grace and fine speech and wondered why she lived alone in the woods. He was about to ask her when a great weariness overcame him and he sank upon the floor in a faint.

Hours later, he awoke to find that he could not move his arms. They were pressed tightly against his sides. And he felt something wet sliding back and forth across his cheek. He looked down and saw—"*Ahhhhhh*"—a huge white snake coiled all around him.

"Who are you?" he asked.

"You do not know?" hissed the snake. "I am the spirit of the snake you killed. I have waited and waited for you. To kill you."

Memories of the pheasant and her babies came suddenly to the man.

"But you were trying to kill tiny birds," he cried. "I didn't want to hurt you. I tried to stop you but you didn't listen. I warned you. Do the same for me."

"All right," hissed the snake. "I'm warning you now. You will be killed. Ready?"

"Not now, wait. Let me go home and bid farewell to my family. I will return. I promise," he begged.

"I have waited too long already," said the snake. But the woodcutter kept on pleading until at last the snake said, "All right. I shall give you one chance. At the top of this mountain is a temple. Near the temple is an old bell. If that bell rings before dawn, I will spare your little life."

The woodcutter had never been to the temple. It was dark, and he was tired. Yet he had to try. He started to stand, but the snake's coils only squeezed him more tightly.

"Nooooo," she whispered. "You do not understand. The bell must ring while you stay here."

That was impossible. The woodcutter now knew that he would die. He said his prayers and prepared for the next world. It was a long and horrible night as the snake slithered all over him, licking his cheek again and again. Finally, the light of dawn crept under the door and the snake raised itself, about to strike.

"*Tang guranggggg*" Suddenly a bell sounded faintly.

"*Sssssssss*" The snake gave a hiss of rage; then with a furious shiver, she turned and slid out the door, robbed of her revenge.

For a long time, the woodcutter did not move, still full of fear. But when after a while the snake had not returned, he tried to move his arms and then slowly stood up.

"Perhaps it was all a dream and there was no snake at all," he thought. "There is only one way to be certain. I must find the bell and see for myself." So he stumbled up the mountain in the morning light, seeking the temple. Pushing through thorns and brush, he finally found it and near it a big bronze bell. But the place was deserted, overgrown with weeds.

A large log hung next to the bell, ready to strike its side, to make it sing. But on that old wooden striker, he saw only dead worms and tired leaves. It hadn't been touched for many years.

"How was the bell rung?" he wondered. "What hit the bell to make it sound?" Slowly, as he puzzled, his eyes fell to the side of the bell and he saw blood. He looked down on the ground and saw more blood, and bits of feather. Then he saw the broken body of a bird. He recognized the mother pheasant he had helped years before.

The woodcutter knelt down beside the bird. His tears wrapped round her body as he thanked her again and again for giving her life. But there was no answer in that blood-red dawn. There was only the silence of the old temple and the stillness of that one kind heart.

National Identity and Pride

10

It may rain gold in a foreign land and stones in your country, but your own country is always better.

—**Malay proverb**

Although some national borders are of recent origin, different Asian countries have had their own history, culture, and identity for many centuries. This identity, the heart of a culture or people, is nourished by the symbols, the images, the history, and the heroes that reflect that culture.

There are legendary heroes, like Tan-gun, the mythical founder of Korea, and heroes of peace, like Gandhi of India or the Dalai Lama of Tibet. There are poets and sages, too: Confucius from China, the wandering poet Basho in Japan, and more. And there are those who struggled for freedom: Rani Lakshmibai of India, who resisted the British in 1857; Muhammad Ali Jinnah, founder of modern Pakistan; Tunku Abdul Rahman, the leader of Malay Independence work, among many.

Epics and myths nourish a sense of national identity, too, both those of one land—the Chinese *Monkey*, *Tum Teav* of Cambodia, and others—as well as the shared epics, like the *Ramayana* and *Mahabharata*, which flow and change across borders. Tales of popular tricksters and favorite comic characters also give a feeling of unity and shared culture, while providing a grand chance to smile.

Silent Debate

KOREA

There are many heroes in Korean history: Admiral Yi Sun-shin, who invented one of the world's first armored boats; Yu Kwan-sun, who defied the Japanese soldiers occupying Korea in the twentieth century, and who died in prison at the age of sixteen; great King Sejong under whose rule many inventions were made. But in folklore, the heroes also can be nameless, like this boatman who never even knew what he did!

Once a Chinese scholar heard of Korea's learned people and went to test the wits of the great thinkers there. After a long, weary trip, he found himself in a boat being ferried toward a large and important Korean city.

As he watched the strong boatman row, he had an idea.

"It is always interesting to find out how clever the working people are in a land," thought the scholar. "Let me test this boatman and see if he has a spark of intelligence." Since the Chinese scholar spoke little Korean, and the Korean boatman knew no Chinese, the scholar decided to converse in a kind of sign language.

Carefully he placed his fingers in the shape of a circle, the symbol of the universe. By this, he wanted to inquire if the boatman knew any of heaven's secrets. Now this boatman spared not a thought about the universe, but instead spent all of his time thinking about the rice cakes which he loved to eat. So when he saw the circle sign, he thought the scholar was asking, "Do you like round rice cakes?"

Well, there was no doubt about that: he liked *all* rice cakes. But he was especially fond of the square kind of rice cake. So to answer, he held up his fingers in the shape of a square, as if to say, "Of course I like round rice cakes, but I prefer the square variety."

The scholar gasped in amazement. For he saw the square as the sign of the earth, and imagined the boatman had replied, "Yes, I know all about the heavens. And I know as well about the earth and its secrets."

Wondering if he had misunderstood, the scholar decided to try one more question. He held up three fingers, as if to say, "Do you know even three of the five important Confucian relationships?"

The boatman, still dreaming of his rice cakes, saw the three fingers and thought, "Ah, he's asking me if I eat three rice cakes at a time." Now this was a silly question, for if you adore rice cakes you never stop with just three. So the boatman quickly held up five fingers, meaning, "Only three? Never. I *always* eat five rice cakes at a time."

The scholar almost fell into the water. For he understood the answer to be, "I know not just three; I understand all five of those important relationships."

"Incredible," whispered the scholar. "This boatman knows so much. If a mere boatman has such learning, then the scholars will be impossible to debate with. They must be truly brilliant. What a land of learning."

Then the Chinese scholar had the boatman turn the boat round and he quickly returned to his own home. He told everyone there about the wondrous learning to be found in Korea. And never again did he try to visit that land of intellectual giants, Korea.

Phù Dô'ng Thiên Vu'o'ng

VIETNAM

Vietnam has had a sad and troubled history, with many invasions and wars over the centuries. One hero to emerge from this turmoil is Phù Dô'ng Thiên Vu'o'ng.

Long ago, the Vietnamese Emperor Hùng Vu'o'ng the Sixth ruled over a peaceful land. Rice fields glowed golden and giving; rivers ran clear and calm. But suddenly, Chinese warriors hungry for power stormed into Vietnam, attacking all who stood in their way. Loyal soldiers rushed to defend their homeland. Many men fought, many men died, but the fighting did not end. In great waves of smoke and blood, the invaders flowed across the land.

Day by day, the Vietnamese army grew weaker and the need for recruits became desperate. From the palace came an imperial order: "*Find more men who will fight.*" Messengers hurried in the four directions, past boys on water buffaloes, through villages circled by bamboo.

One such messenger soon arrived in Phù Dô'ng, a village near the northern border. Eager to help, the village crier there ran by starfruit trees, his voice leaping from a bamboo tube as he spread the appeal.

"Who will go fight, I wonder?" sighed an older man as he listened.

"It is no concern of ours. We have enough to do," answered his wife, fanning their only son, Gióng. And they did have enough, for their son was a different sort of child. Never in his three years had he said one word, walked one step, or even crawled. The elder parents spent their days worried about their son's future. Now they both gazed fondly at the child while he lay, as always, silent and still in his rattan cradle.

Then all of a sudden, after hearing the crier's voice, Gióng seemed to waken from a long, long sleep. For the first time, he raised himself up. For the first time, he stood on his legs. For the first time, sounds came from his silent lips.

"Please invite the imperial messenger here, my parents. I wish to speak to him," he declared in a loud, powerful voice. His parents stared, amazed at their child.

"My son, you can stand!" cried his mother. "You can talk! How can this be?"

"Bring the messenger here, for I have more to say," replied Gióng calmly. Bewildered by the change in the boy, the father ran off and soon returned with the emperor's servant.

"I can help to fight our country's enemies," said the boy. "But I will need an iron horse, an iron rod, armor, and much food."

The boy spoke well, with true confidence and strength. Even though he was little, it was easy to believe him, to trust his words. So the messenger, much impressed, agreed to take the boy's requests to the emperor.

Full of hope, he raced toward the palace and past golden dragons to enter the grand doors. Through the palace he moved until he stood beneath the emperor's throne. Bowing at the bottom of its nine steps, he waited respectfully. Finally, brass drums and gongs sounded, permitting him to speak. His eyes still lowered, the messenger began to talk. "Respected Highness, a most unusual boy of three years, who speaks like a hero indeed, offers to fight the invading army. But he needs an iron horse, an iron rod, armor, and much food."

Gravely, the emperor listened, for he in his wisdom knew that all, big and small, can help their country. After a few moments, he agreed to the boy's strange requests.

Orders flew to the imperial warehouse: "Melt down all of your iron." Gifts of more metal poured in as people throughout Vietnam heard of young Gióng's courage. Blacksmiths from across the land came to help. Fires roared as iron was melted in great pots then pounded into strong new shapes. In days, a fierce iron horse, a sturdy iron rod, and an invincible set of armor stood ready.

Back in Phù Dô'ng village, people were also busy. All day, every day, they fed the boy.

Rice, vegetables, and meats were brought, piled in brass

bowls or wrapped in banana leaves. Delicious smells danced around Gióng as he ate and ate, then grew and grew into a true giant. Soon, he towered over his mother, his father, and all of the villagers.

"Can this be the same little boy who never moved for three years?" his neighbors asked each other as they stared up at him.

"Perhaps the spirits above have sent him to help our beloved land," the wisest villager whispered.

At last, the iron horse, the rod, and the armor were brought to the giant Gióng. He stepped into the armor, grasped the rod, and jumped easily onto the horse. Feeling the touch of brave Gióng, the iron horse reared up and together they flew off to fight.

With fire blazing from his horse, Gióng roared into the midst of the enemy, swinging his rod in fury. Enemy spears melted and men dropped like ripe figs from trees. Arrows flew toward Gióng but fell featherlike from his horse. Soldiers ran away, shaking in fear.

Watching this hero, Vietnamese fighters now battled with increased strength and hope. Then suddenly, Gióng's iron rod broke in two. At once he raced to a nearby range of bamboo and ripped a huge pole from the earth. Waving his new weapon, he cut a path through the enemy. Eyes wide, hearts pounding, the invaders lost all desire to fight, and instead fled back over the border. Overjoyed at the victory, the Vietnamese fighters rushed to surround and cheer their hero. But he was no longer in their midst.

"There he goes," someone cried. "He's leaving us!"

Everyone stared across the fields as the giant on the iron horse sped away. Over the grass leapt the two, to the top of Sóc-so'n mountain. On they flew, higher and higher, until only their shadow lingered on a cloud.

That was the last time anyone saw Gióng. Some say that he returned to the heavens, reporting back to the Jade Emperor who sent him here. But no one knows for sure. The Vietnamese Emperor renamed the boy, to honor his memory. He called him Phù Dô'ng Thiên Vu'o'ng—God's Messenger from Phù Dô'ng village.

Years later, a large footprint on a rock was found at the top of Sóc-so'n mountain. Temples in his name were built near the rock and in the surrounding areas. Even today, many people visit these temples yearly to thank Phù Dô'ng Thiên Vu'o'ng, who saved their beautiful land. And so it is that Vietnamese everywhere, even those far from their beloved homeland, still remember him with pride, and tell his story with respect.

A Chey

CAMBODIA

Cambodia, a land which has faced more sorrow than most in recent years, has also many tales of wit and several well-known tricksters. Judge Rabbit remains a beloved character, as does the boy A Chey, who tricks his master, the king, and even the Emperor of China in tale after tale.

Once in Cambodia, there lived a very clever young boy named A Chey. He played so many tricks, so well, that his master soon wished to be rid of him. One day, he decided to take A Chey to the king and to leave him there. The two journeyed past pagodas and rice fields and at last saw the sparkling roof of the king's grand palace. In they walked through jasmine scent, past fine painted walls. Hands together in greeting, they bowed before the king. The merchant then boasted of the boy's wit and suggested that A Chey stay in the palace for some time.

"A Chey, they say that you are clever. Can you tell me a big lie?" the king asked the ten-year-old boy.

"Perhaps I could, your respected highness," answered A Chey. "But not now, for I need my *Book of Lies* which is at my house."

A servant was sent to bring the book back. He rode through bamboo to the mother's small home.

"Give me A Chey's *Book of Lies* at once," he ordered. The poor woman was scared and confused.

"I have never heard of it. There must be some mistake. It is not here, I'm certain," she said. The two searched everywhere but the book was not found. Fearfully, the servant returned and reported his failure.

"What is the meaning of this?" demanded the king angrily to A Chey. "Where is the book? I want it here now, so that you can try to trick me and tell me a lie."

"Forgive me, sir," said A Chey with a bow. "But I have just played my first trick on you. I lied about the *Book of Lies* and you believed me. You even sent a servant to bring it. But of course he couldn't find it, because there is no such book anywhere."

The king looked most annoyed for a moment, but then he smiled and allowed A Chey to stay. So the boy moved into the palace and there he lived for a long time, playing trick after trick after trick.

The Zither-Met Friends

CHINA

Symbols of national pride and identity are varied, including a food like Korean kimchee, an animal such as the Indian cow, or even a weapon like the kris of the Malay people. For the Chinese, the zither, known since the Bronze age, is very special. Kate Stevens describes it: "The body is of wood, covered with layer upon layer of lacquer; long, low, and narrowly rectangular. The silken strings hug the sound box closely, producing a quiet intimate sound. It is an instrument of introspection—played alone or for a few close friends. The player is seated before a table on which the instrument is placed; incense is burnt; emotions are calmed."

Stories about the zither abound. This one is especially interesting in that it offers a test of Chinese history and tradition, while also providing a model of true friendship. The tale is from a version by Kate Stevens, beginning with the first two lines as she heard them in a Taiwan teahouse forty years ago.

Translation:
Lords of the Warring States—great the turmoil;
It brought forth sages and famous men.

One such a man was Yu Boya, an official of the State of Jin. The Lord of Jin sent him on a mission to the State of Chu, and when that mission was complete, Yu Boya boarded his official boat and began the journey, by river, back to Jin. The boat had just reached the Han Yang River when a storm delayed them, and they anchored, as dark clouds spread over the sky and rain soaked down. When the sky cleared and the rain ceased, Yu Boya threw open his cabin window and looked out upon the river scene. It was Mid-Autumn Festival, and in the light of the full moon he saw the river waves, like myriad silver snakes tumbling one over the other. On the river bank, the cassia trees gave forth their scent, and the dying notes of the cicadas, insects of autumn, could be heard. And Yu Boya was seized by a change of mood.

"Come," he called to his servant. "Set out my zither for I would play and dispell my melancholy." And so, in the full light of the moon, amid the yellowing autumn grasses, Yu Boya began to play.

As the official began to play, there came along the riverbank a woodcutter, Zhong Ziqi. He had once been an official himself, but because his parents were old, with no one to care for them, he had come back home. Now he lived with his parents in Gathering of Sages Village, and every day he went into the mountains for firewood, which he sold at the market to provide their livelihood. He was returning home when he, too, was delayed by the storm. But when the sky cleared and the rain ceased, Zhong Ziqi once again took up his load of firewood and headed along the riverbank to home, when suddenly he heard the sound of a zither. Transfixed, he set down his burden and listened. The melody was a lament for the disciple of Confucius, Yan Hui, so lofty of talent and of such short life span. And as the woodcutter listened, suddenly one of the zither strings snapped in two.

"Ahh." The official, Yu Boya, was startled almost out of his wits. "There must be a hidden listener." But the boatmen said there was no settlement nearby—nothing but wooded bank and river water. "Then," said Yu Boya to his servant, "you must go and search the riverbank rushes, for surely some bandit lurks there."

With that, the woodcutter stepped forward. "No need for any search. It is only I, a humble woodcutter, listening to your zither."

"Ha, ha, ha." Yu Boya's laugh was scornful. "Listening to my zither! The zither is an instrument of China's scholars; how dare a woodcutter claim to be a listener? Ha! Ha! Ha!"

But Zhong Ziqi spoke up again, quite calmly. "I seem to remember that the zither has six taboos, eight excellences, and seven never-plays. If you had no listener, you, sir, should not have played."

Yu Boya was taken aback. "Let me not take this woodcutter too lightly; perhaps even by these hills and streams there are those with some knowledge."

"Go," he called to his servant, "bring this woodcutter aboard; I would speak to him of the zither."

Down the gangplank went the servant and approached Zhong Ziqi. "When you see my master, be sure to kowtow. Whatever he asks you, answer carefully and clearly." Up the gangplank strode Zhong Ziqi, the woodcutter, and when he approached Yu Boya, he gave the salute of equals, "At your service, sir."

"Sit over there," said Yu Boya, afraid of losing his official dignity, and he did not even have tea brought. "I have a few questions to ask you, since you call yourself a connoiseur of the zither."

"Oh sir," replied the woodcutter, "what I know is all too little; pray do not measure me by your capacity."

"My questions are simple and few," said Yu Boya.

Who was it first handed down the zither?
Where handed down? Whence came its name?
Of what wood is a zither fashioned?
Who made the zither that I play now?
If each word and answer is correct,
True, woodcutter, you are a listener.

And the woodcutter replied:

The first zither was made by the god Fu Xi,
Handed down at Jaspar Pool; we call it Jaspar Zither.
To make a zither, use paulownia wood,
Top part too light, base part too dense—
Choose a center piece for perfect balance.
There once was a master craftsman, Liu Ziqi,
It was he who made your zither.

"That is all correct," said Yu Boya. "But I have a few more questions:

What is the width of the zither's head?
How narrow the tail? Why so determined?
How many the inlaid studs, and why?
How many elements? How many tones?
The lines of lacquer crackle—
What do they reflect?
How many feet, inches, and tenths?
Who loved virtue?
Who loved war?
How many strings are there in all?
If each word and answer is correct,
True, woodcutter, you are a listener.

And once again the wood cutter replied:

The width at the head—eight inches across,
The tail four inches, to mark the four seasons.
The inlaid studs, like the months, are twelve
Plus an intercalary; Five Elements mean Five Tones.
The lines of lacquer crackle match the earth's orbit,
Three feet, six inches, and five tenths in length.
King Wen loved virtue, King Wu loved war;
Each added a string for a total of seven.
When the notes pierce the heavens, paired phoenixes rejoice;
When the sounds reach hill and sea, tiger and dragon are kin.

"Each word and answer is correct," said Yu Boya. "But do you know what was the theme of the music I played?"

"It was a lament," answered Zhong Ziqi, "for the disciple of Confucius, Yan Hui, lofty of talent and of such brief life span. You wove the moonlight and the autumn water into this piece."

"Wonderful! wonderful!" exclaimed Yu Boya. "Truly you are a listener, a connoiseur of the zither." With that he had a banquet set out, and that very night they swore eternal brotherhood, having met over the zither. Long they talked into the night, but when dawn came Yu Boya, in duty bound, went on his way homeward to Jin. And much as the official wanted to take the woodcutter back to court with him, Zhong Ziqi must remain with his aged parents. So the two friends parted, agreeing to meet again at this very bank one year hence, at the next Autumn Moon Festival.

A year went by, and Yu Boya returned to that bank on the Han Yang River. He looked for his friend, but Zhong Ziqi did not appear. "Perhaps he has been delayed," thought Yu Boya, and he set out his zither and began to play. Still Zhong Ziqi did not appear.

"Strange," said Yu Boya. "Can he have mistaken the day? Come!" he commanded his servant. "Bring my zither; we will go to my friend's village." So the two set out along the path that led away from the riverbank. They had gone only a little way when they came to a fork in the path; which way to go? As they hesitated, an old man came down one fork of the path towards them.

"Sir," said Yu Boya, "can you tell me the way to Gathering of Sages Village?"

"Do you want the Upper or Lower Village?" asked the old man.

"That I do not know," replied Yu Boya. "But I have come in search of my friend, Zhong Ziqi."

Then the old man was silent for a time; tears filled his eyes. "You must be Yu Boya. My son, on his deathbed, commanded me to bury him on the headland overlooking the river, so that he would not fail his appointment with you."

"Take me to his grave," said Yu Boya. When they reached the grave, Yu Boya burned incense and set out his zither. He played a lament for his friend who had understood his playing as no one else had ever done, a lament for his friend lost so soon after meeting. And when the lament was over, he took his priceless zither and smashed it into a thousand pieces there at the grave. It was his way to requite his listener.

And to this day, when Chinese wish to describe a special friend, the one who truly understands you, they say, *zhiyin*, listener, one who hears the heart's music.

José Rizal

PHILIPPINES

José Rizal was an exceptional human being who remains a source of pride to this day for Filipinos everywhere. To do justice to the many talents he had, one would need a large space and much time. Here, I give the bare facts of his life, and excerpts from his famous farewell poem, for you to piece together and share with others.

José Rizal was born June 19, 1861, to a happy, cultured family, but in a land ruled by Spain. First taught at home, writing poems by eight, he later excelled in school, showing artistic talent as well as kindness. In his early years, he was rather weak physically, but he gained strength through daily walks and gymnastics. As an adult, he learned to handle a sword with skill.

José knew injustice early in life when his mother was arrested and jailed for two and a half years on a false charge. To him, this was yet another example of power wrongly wielded by Spanish rulers, and one well remembered when he left for further study in Europe.

In Spain, and elsewhere in Europe, Rizal studied medicine, watched life around him, discussed politics with new friends, and wrote his first novel, *Noli Me Tangere* (*The Social Cancer*). When published, at great hardship to Rizal, it was an immediate sensation—hated by the Spanish, admired by the Filipinos and their supporters. Showing Filipinos as people with wisdom, honesty, and courage, the book was banned in the Philippines, and his family was persecuted.

Rizal became a medical doctor, specializing in diseases of the eyes, for his country needed that knowledge. He was pleased when he helped improve his mother's fading eyesight.

Because of his outspoken criticism, though, it was not wise for him to live in his homeland. He visited his beloved land, but then went abroad again, this time to Hong Kong, the U.S., and Europe. When in England, he translated an important early history which proved that before the Spanish came, the Philippines were islands of energy, art, and progress. Through his writings, including a second novel, *El Filibusterismo* (*The Reign of Greed*), he urged people to think of freedom, showing them the terrible price his country had paid under Spanish rule.

Rizal's words influenced countless readers and his medical skill healed many, yet he was also a talented sculptor, painter, and a translator who spoke a number of European and Asian languages fluently. These gifts meant little to the Spanish rulers of the Philippines and in 1892, after his return, he was deported to the small island of Dapitan. Even there, in this quiet, forgotten place, he made great changes: creating street lighting with coconut oil lamps, starting a waterworks and a school, building a hospital, writing, and sending valuable collections of plant and animal samples to European scientists.

For his energetic work, he earned the hatred of many Spaniards, who plotted against him. At last, their efforts resulted in his arrest for treason. In a quick trial with a judge but no justice, he was found guilty.

Several days later, on December 30, 1896, innocent but accepting this final indignity, José Rizal said farewell to his family. Soon after, he marched out to stand before a firing squad. He asked to be shot in the head, facing the squad, but his request was denied. He was ordered to turn, to be shot in the back as a traitor. Yet his will was so strong that after the shots had been fired, he twisted his body as he fell. Thus he died with his face looking up at the bright sky above the land he loved.

The Spanish watchers who came to celebrate his death now thought themselves safe in their power. They were not. The death of José Rizal inspired his countrypeople to further resist the colonialists. Two years after his death, the Spanish flag was lowered forever over the Philippines.

Rizal's writings are known by all in the Philippines. His last poem, "Mi Ultimo Adios" ("My Last Farewell"), written on the eve of his execution and smuggled out to his sister, has been translated into many languages. The excerpts here were read to the U.S. Congress decades ago to gain American support for Filipino freedom; even today, they show the spirit of a hero.

> *... my ashes shall at last be one with thy hills and thy valleys.*
> *Little 'twill matter, then, my country, that thou shouldst forget me!*
> *I shall be air in thy streets, and I shall be space in thy meadows;*
> *I shall be vibrant speech in thine ears, shall be fragrance and color,*
> *Light and shout, and loved song, forever repeating my message.*
>
> *Idolized fatherland, thou crown and deep of my sorrows,*
> *Lovely Philippine Isles, once again adieu! I am leaving*
> *All with thee—my friends, my love. Where I go there are no tyrants;*
> *There one dies not for the cause of his faith; there God is the ruler.*
> *Farewell, father and mother and brother, dear friends of the fireside!*
> *Thankful ye should be for me that I rest at the end of the long day ...* [1]

Wit and Wisdom 11

One who can turn the tongue can turn the world.
—**Cambodian saying**

A rich tradition of laughter is found across Asia. Even in countries torn by war again and again, stories of tricksters, of fools, of witty men and women are widely found. Humor has always been one way to relieve tensions, to get back at others. In older times, stories of foolish scholars, magistrates, and officials helped those at the bottom of strict hierarchies to ridicule those at the top. Today, the modern joke eases the stress of a faster, more complicated urban lifestyle.

Humor does not always move easily across borders. Tales about women told to me by some male Japanese would not be funny to many Western women. And my Indian husband was horrified when an American friend playfully teased him at our wedding, saying, "Best of luck, but if doesn't work out, divorce is easy nowadays."

Puns and word play, which figure so prominently in humor, are almost impossible to use across linguistic borders. And the sophisticated asides and topical comments that spice up storytelling styles like rakugo or Harikatha rarely get translated. Even so, there's still quite a bit to laugh about.

Tricksters and Fools

Andare

Sri Lanka

Andare is a trickster well known to Sri Lankans. From this trick has come a saying: Andare gala issuva vageyi *("Like Andare's attempt to move the stone").*

One day Andare walked down a quiet path and suddenly heard a sigh. He saw a most discouraged farmer staring at a huge rock.

"Ah, this rock," he said as Andare stopped near him, "it is too large. I have trouble plowing around it."

"If you feed me well for a month, I can move that with ease," offered Andare. The farmer was delighted and so for four weeks, Andare grew plump on the farmer's soft rice and spicy sauces. Meanwhile, like smoke, the news of his boast spread through the village. Around the well and in the market streets, people talked only of the giant who had such strength. They waited eagerly for the end of the month, when he would move the rock. At last that day arrived. Andare, fresh from his oil bath and looking very strong, strode up to the rock. He greeted the large crowd watching him and thanked the farmer for his fine food.

Slowly, he took a deep breath. Then he bent over at the waist, with his hands resting on his knees, his back flat, ready for a load.

"Now," he shouted to the crowd, "if someone will just put the rock on my back, then I'll move it as I promised."

Xieng Mieng

LAOS

In Laos, Xieng Mieng is a very popular trickster who deceives both farmers and the king.

One day the king, feeling quite bored, offered a reward to the person who could bring him the most delicious food. Various delicacies were prepared yet none pleased him. Then Xieng Mieng came and said, "Tonight, I shall bring you the best food. But your tongue must be perfectly clear to taste it. Please eat nothing until I return."

The king agreed and sat without eating for hours, dreaming of the wonderful food soon to come. Meanwhile, Xieng Mieng slept and slept, then finally boiled plain white rice.

When it was very dark and very late, he walked slowly to the palace, carrying a bowl of rice. The king was waiting eagerly. He was starving for he had not eaten all day.

"Why are you so late?" demanded the king. "And where is your delicious food?" Xieng Mieng bowed low and held out the rice.

"But this is only plain rice," said the king.

"Taste it, please, sir," said clever Xieng Mieng. Since his stomach was so empty, the king ate every grain of rice. When he finished, he gave a sigh of pleasure. Plain rice indeed tasted simply delicious to a hungry man. The king rewarded Xieng Mieng, then went to bed much satisfied and wiser as well.

Hodja

INDIA

Stories of Hodja's wit long have traveled throughout the world. His tales still are shared in many Muslim areas of Asia, and are enjoyed by nonMuslims as well.

Once a bully loudly bragged of his strength and constantly showed off in Hodja's village. So Hodja decided to teach him a lesson. One hot day, he walked up to the bully while the man was exercising.

"I have heard that you have the strength of ten men," said Hodja.

"Perhaps even more," sneered the bully. "Certainly more than you, my short little man."

"Then let us have a contest tomorrow," challenged Hodja. "We will invite a crowd to watch and they can decide who is stronger."

The bully laughed a hard, mean laugh and easily agreed, certain of victory. He spent the night boasting about how easily he would beat Hodja. Late the next morning, many people gathered to see the contest.

Hodja marched up to the bully and held out a handkerchief. He pointed to a nearby wall. "The winner of our match is the one who can throw this cloth over that wall."

"Surely you joke," said the bully. "This is too easy." With a lazy grin, he took the cloth and tossed it toward the wall. But it fluttered down at his feet. He picked it up, crushed it into a ball and threw it even harder. But again, it floated gently down near his toe. His face a bit red, he tried again, and again, and again. Yet the cloth never went farther than a foot or two.

"It is my turn now," said Hodja, and the bully angrily gave him the handkerchief. Hodja bent down and picked up a stone.

He put it carefully in the middle of the cloth, then tied a knot around it. Holding the cloth firmly, he took a deep breath and threw it. It sailed easily above the crowd and over the wall.

Everyone cheered and laughed with delight, for no one likes a bully. Hodja was declared the winner and he walked happily away, surrounded by friends. The bully, feeling quite foolish, stood all alone. Soon after that, he left the village, and he never returned.

Si Kabayan

INDONESIA

In Indonesia and Malaysia, the little mousedeer is a famous trickster. In West Java, the popular Si Kabayan can seem either very clever or *very foolish.*

Si Kabayan sat crying one day and a friend came up to ask why.

"Because I have a new shirt on," sobbed Si Kabayan.

"But that's good news," said the friend. "Why would that make you cry?"

"Because it will get old!"

WORD PLAY

Some Asian languages are tonal and offer possibilities for word play unknown in English. A word in Vietnamese may be spoken six different ways to make six different meanings. In Chinese, there are delightful pun stories which play off of the many meanings of one word inflected differently. Even in Korean, Japanese, and other atonal languages of Asia, the possibility for word play exists: When a storm threatens a Korean boat, those on board use their different learnings to try to stop it. The one who succeeds is the physician because he recites a healing chant for the stomach (bae) in hopes that it will work well for a boat, also bae. It does!

Ainu Wit

AINU PEOPLE OF JAPAN

One day, a much respected Ainu scholar, Kyosuke Kindaichi, sat talking with another Ainu speaker, Seitaroe Kaizawa. He asked him, "What three words of great importance to the Ainu have the same suffix?" Kaizawa instantly replied, "*Noype, sanpe, parunpe* (brain, heart, tongue)."

The professor smiled and said right back, "How about: "*siretok, rametok, pawetok?* (beauty, courage, eloquence)"—the characteristics of ideal men for Ainu. Both men laughed, well pleased and well matched in wit.[1]

The Sky is Dark, is Dark

TAIWAN

Songs and chants are often found in Asian stories or in storytelling sessions. This folk song from Taiwan, kindly translated by Joanna C. Yu, plays with words and repetition to give a humorous picture.

The sky is dark, is dark;
it's about to rain, to rain.
The old man takes his hoe, to search some roots.
He digs, he digs;
he finds an eel?
Oh, this is so funny.

The old man wants it cooked salty;
the old woman wants it cooked light.
The old man wants it cooked salty;
the old woman wants it cooked light.
The two fight, and break the wok,
kin-kon, kin-kon.
Ha, ha, ha, this is so funny.

Endless Tale

JAPAN

Endless tales are another form of word play. And they can be old and new. Recently in a Korean storytelling class, a young mother told of her father, a great storyteller. When children pestered him for too many stories, he would tell them how he climbed a tall hill then pushed a steel watermelon down that kept rolling and rolling and rolling and rolling (until they cried Stop!). In Japan, there are many, many endless tales as well.

Long ago, in a rich man's rice storehouse, many, many mice lived. They kept coming and going. First, a mouse crawled outside, *choro choro.* Then another followed, *choro choro.* Then another went out, *choro choro.* One more crawled out, *choro choro.* Another left, *choro choro,* and another, *choro choro,* and the next, *choro choro,* and the next, and the next, and the next ...

The Ceremony

Blended Cultures

Many true, funny tales involve words, meanings, and their transformation across language and culture. Here is one from my own life.

When I was pregnant with our son, my husband and I tried to take the best advice from East and West. I drank milk with saffron for a bright child, as our Indian relatives suggested. I wore a charm for safe childbirth sent from Japan, and I listened to my Italian aunts as well.

Then one day, my husband returned from the local Sears parking lot where he had met an Indian friend, Yasha.

"Yasha wants to help, to do a ceremony for you," he said. "It involves some special bath. It has a strange name."

"An Indian bath? Before the baby is born? Or after? At home or in the hospital?" I asked.

"I don't know all the details," he said. "It must be some North Indian custom. I suppose they pour water on your hands or something, maybe to purify you."

"Well, do I need to fast, or do anything to prepare myself?" I continued.

"I'm not sure," replied my husband, a bit annoyed. "Yasha is from North India; I'm from the South. I don't know much about their customs. I think she said people would bring gifts. In India, we usually bring coconuts or flowers or bananas for ceremonies. Maybe that's what they'll bring here."

Suddenly something clicked inside my head. Thoughts of incense, coconuts, temple bells, and Indian rituals vanished.

"Wait a minute," I said. "This ceremony, is it called a shower?"

"Yes! That's it!" he cried happily. "That's the strange name. A baby shower. Yasha wants to give you a baby shower!"

WISDOM

A Costly Smell

BURMA

Tales of judges and wise decisions are popular across Asia. At times, the judge works in secret, as does Park Moon Su, a secret inspector in Korea. Other times, he might be a wise grandfather figure, like Judge Ooka of Japan, whose cases make fine problems for students. An interesting female judge is Princess Learned-in-the-Law of Burma.

One busy market day, a poor traveler sat down to eat his meal of rice and vegetables. As he ate, the fine odors of a nearby fish stall, blown by the wind, soon surrounded him. He chewed slowly, enjoying the smells, pretending he was eating good, costly fish instead of his plain meal. When he was finished, the owner of the fish stall suddenly came up.

"That will be one silver coin," she demanded.

"But I ate nothing of yours," said the traveler.

"You sampled the smells from my fish," she replied. "So you should pay." He refused. They argued and argued until at last they went before Princess Learned-in-the-Law.

She carefully questioned them both and heard each of their arguments. She closed her eyes for a moment and then spoke.

"The traveler did indeed use and enjoy the smell of your fine fish, and thus he must pay," she said. The traveler looked at her sadly, feeling her most unfair, while the fish seller beamed.

"What is the price of your best fish?" the judge asked the woman.

"One silver coin," she replied happily.

"This will be the method of payment," continued Princess Learned-in-the-Law. "You two must go outside. There the traveler will hold out one silver coin. Let the woman then take the shadow it makes. For if the price of a fish is a silver coin, then the price of the smell of a fish is the shadow of a silver coin."

A Woman's Wit

NEPAL

Although women, until recently, have traditionally had more limited options and opportunities in Asia, a number of stories recount their wisdom, courage, and strength.

Once in Nepal, a poor bamboo cutter heard a voice as he worked in the forest.

"Come deeper and find the best bamboo," it said over and over. It was a fine, strong voice.

"I would like to find better bamboo, to make a little money," thought the man. As he heard the words again and again, they seemed to cast a spell upon him and he walked farther into the shadowy woods.

"Now I have that silly man under my power," thought the voice, which belonged to a rather hungry monster. "Let him walk around here in a trance, while I go eat his tasty wife and children. Then I'll come back and have him for dessert."

In seconds, the monster used his power and made himself look just like the bamboo cutter. He went to the man's house and ate a simple meal prepared by the wife. She put the children to sleep, and then, as she was putting down the mats to go to bed, she noticed her husband's feet. They were turned around—the toes in back and the heels in front. All at once, she realized that this was not her kind husband, but rather an evil monster. Yet she didn't show her fear and she quickly thought of a plan.

As soon as he was sleeping, she crawled away, leaving a pillow to look like her body. She took her two children, putting two more pillows in their place. Then she scattered some slippery peas and climbed quietly down from the sleeping loft. She removed the ladder, made certain that the fire was hot under the loft, then ran away to hide.

After some time, the monster awoke very hungry and bit eagerly into the woman next to him.

"Ahhhh!" he shouted, spitting out feathers. "Where is she? Well, at least the children will be good for a bite." And he bit, hard, into another pillow.

With feathers floating all over, he stood up in the dark, looking very silly. In a rage, he started after the woman. But he slipped on the peas, and when he stepped down for the ladder, he tumbled right into the fire. There was soon little left of that mean monster.

When all was quiet, the wife crept back and saw the body.

"Ahh," she said, "now I must get rid of it. But how?" Next to her was a fine big chest. She opened it and managed to push the corpse inside. She left her door wide open, and the chest in plain sight. Then she and the children hid in the loft.

That night, some robbers came by and saw the open door.

"That will be an easy place to rob," said the leader. "Follow me." Inside they crept and found a fine heavy chest.

"This must be loaded with household treasures," whispered the clever robber leader. "Let us take it now and open it later on." So the robbers struggled, pushing and pulling, and with great difficulty carried the chest back to their hide-out.

"Is it be gold or silver or silks?" wondered a robber as he took an ax and broke the lock. Eagerly, they all peered inside.

"*Aaaahhhh*!" They jumped back when they saw the huge teeth, the enormous tongue, and the ugly staring eyes of a great, dead monster. They ran away as fast as they could, and were so scared that they never stole again.

As for the woman, after she saw the robbers take her chest, she went down and locked the door tightly, then fell into a deep sleep. In the morning, when her husband had still not returned, she went after him. She found him wandering in the forest, staring ahead with a strange look. Taking his hand, she pulled him away. As soon as they left the woods, the spell was over.

"Why are you here with me, good wife?" asked the man, much confused. She told him all the adventures of the night.

"How clever of you," he said at last. They returned home happily and the whole family had a grand meal to celebrate their good fortune in just being alive.

MODERN JOKES AND STORIES

The modern Asian joke is quite democratic in its reach, commenting on rioting students in Korea, the political situation in China, telephones in India, honeymooners in Japan, beginning English speakers in Malaysia, the country bumpkin visiting Bangkok, and so much more. Here are several recent Asian favorites.

Momma, the Little Crab is Snapping my Finger

THAILAND

The growth in Asian cities has been astounding. But as many people have left the countryside seeking jobs, they have often increased urban problems of transportation, sanitation, housing, and employment. Another result of urbanization (and the growing strength of national media) is the standardization of culture, including language. Rich, regional differences get brushed aside and a person's speech provoke or reveal prejudice, as in this tale I received from Wajuppa Tossa.

Once a girl from the northeast of Thailand (Isan) went to work in Bangkok. She learned to speak central Thai, to dress like people from Bangkok, to eat central Thai food. However, she missed her family after living in Bangkok for a few years. So she asked her boss for a home leave.

When she was at home, she refused to speak Lao, the major dialect of her village. She kept speaking Bangkok Thai, to show off.

One day, she was hungry so she asked her mother: "Mother, I am very hungry. Do you have anything for me to eat?"

Mother could not understand her. So she asked, "Why don't you speak Lao? I don't understand."

The girl said, "Oh, I can't speak Lao any more, Mother. What do you have for me to eat? Eat, you know, put food in your mouth and it goes to your stomach."

So Mother brought out some live crabs to show her daughter. "Here, Daughter, I have some crabs; we can make steamed crabs."

The girl pointed at a live crab and asked, "Mother, what do you call this?"

Mother did not even have a chance to answer when the crab snapped the girl's finger. So she screamed, clearly, in Lao:

"Momma, *the little crab* is snapping my finger. *Help!*"

Amazing Indian Trains

INDIA

A man in Chennai got on a sleeper train car bound for Delhi. He walked into a first class compartment with four bunk beds, two on each side. He climbed onto the top bunk, which he had reserved. For a while he slept, but at midnight when the train stopped at a large station, he awoke and stepped off the train for tea. As he sipped sleepily, he heard the whistle. Quickly he stumbled into a train at the platform and found a sleeping compartment that looked like his in the dark. However, this train was going from Delhi to Chennai, taking him right back home.

The train began to move and he tried to sleep. But he remained wide awake, listening to all the sounds. After a while, he heard the man in the bottom bunk sit up, so he called down, "Are you going to Delhi, too, or getting off before?"

"Delhi? Not at all," answered the man. "I'm going straight to Chennai right now."

"Ah," sighed the man in the top bunk, "our Indian trains are truly amazing, aren't they? Top bunk goes to Delhi, while bottom bunk goes to Chennai!"

Chasing the Monkeys

INDIA

When a new Satellite Research Centre started in Bangalore, it was very close to the forest. The monkeys who lived in the nearby woods constantly annoyed those at the Centre, so the Government spent much money vainly trying to drive them away.

One day, a scientist told the chief officer, "I can drive them away very simply." He asked for a fee, which the officer promised reluctantly, since he had already spent much money on the monkey menace!

This fellow went and said something to the herd of monkeys. All the monkeys started laughing. Then he said something else. All the monkeys cried. Finally he said a few more words and they all ran off!

The chief officer called to him, "It worked. But what did you say?"

"I told them that I worked at the Satellite Centre, and they all laughed," replied the scientist. "Then I told them what I'm paid, and they all cried over my poor salary."

"And what made the monkeys leave?" asked the officer seriously.

"I asked, 'Will you join our organisation?' and suddenly all the monkeys ran away!"

NOTES

In these notes, I've included motifs from Stith Thompson's *Motif-Index of Folk Literature* and folktale types from Antti Aarne's and Thompson's classic guide. In tracking down story variants, motifs, and types, I have also referred to the several adaptations of these works using early Asian folklore collections, and to Margaret Read MacDonald's very helpful *The Storyteller's Sourcebook.*

Also useful were two guides by Asian folklore scholars: *The Yanagita Kunio Guide to the Japanese Folk Tale* and In-hak Choi's *A Type Index of Korean Folktales.* However, since all such motifs and types are based on folklore, I have not listed them for any of the true stories.

INTRODUCTION

References

1. Dharampal, *Indian Science and Technology in the Eighteenth Century* (Delhi: Impex India, 1971), lxi.

2. Claude Alvares, "The Genius of Hindu Civilization," *Illustrated Weekly of India,* June 15, 1986, 9.

3. John Naisbitt, *Megatrends Asia* (New York: Simon & Schuster, 1996), 237.

4. http://irdu.nus.sg/kampungnet/main.html.

CHAPTER 1: **Storytellers and Styles**

References

1. Kate Stevens, "The World of the Chinese Storyteller," *Appleseed Quarterly* 7 (Spring 1997): 22.

CHAPTER 2: **Storytelling Tools**

References

1. Woo Ok Kim, "P'ansori: An Indigenous Theater of Korea" (Ph.D. diss., New York University, 1980), 147.

2. Catherine Stevens, "Peking Drumsinging" (Ph.D. diss., Harvard University, 1972), 238.

3. Stevens, "Peking Drumsinging," 239.

4. K.B. Das and L.K. Mahapatra, *Folklore of Orissa* (New Delhi: National Book Trust, 1979), 148.

5. Aung San Suu Kyi, *Freedom From Fear* (New York: Viking Penguin, 1991), 246.

6. Ban-song Song, "Kwangdae Ka: A Source Material for the P'ansori Tradition," *Korea Journal* 16 (Aug. 1976): 26.

7. Kate Stevens, "The World of the Chinese Storyteller," *Appleseed Quarterly* 7 (Spring 1997): 18.

8. Marshall Pihl, *The Korean Singer of Tales* (Cambridge: Harvard University Press, 1994), 91.

9. Sally Peterson, "Translating Experience and the Reading of a Story Cloth," *Journal of American Folklore* 101 (Jan.-Mar. 1988): 15.

10. Stevens, "The World of the Chinese Storyteller," 18.

CHAPTER 3: **Harmony and Friendship**

Two Friends

This little teaching tale was told to me in 1987 by Blia Xiong, a leader of the Hmong community in Seattle. It is also found in Vang and Lewis, *Grandmother's Path*, 19, while Thompson lists Halm, *Aesop* #311, as a source (*Motif Index* 4: 117).

Motifs include J1488. What the bear whispered in his ear; W121. Cowardice. Type 179: What bear whispered in ear.

Yamanba of the Mountain

Tales of yamanba abound in Japan, although most yamanba are not as kind as this one. I heard her story during a wonderful overnight of storytellers from northern Kyushu island in 1993, organized by a dear friend, Keiko Shirane. As we sat around the woodstove in a log home circled by mountains, we shared many tales, including this from a teller born in northern Tohoku. The story is told as a picturebook (Matsutani, *Yamanba no Fushiki*) and also as a kamishibai storycard set: *Chofuku Yama no Yamanba* by Hiroya Nose (Tokyo: NHK Service Center, 1984).

Motifs include D855.5. Magic object as reward for good deeds; D1652.8. Inexhaustible cloth; G284. Witch as helper; P310. Friendship.

Himsuka

I heard this in 1970 from my friend Ram Swarup, a gentle scholar in Delhi who arises at 4:00 each morning for yoga and meditation. He knows many stories, especially from his Hindu heritage, and loves to share them simply. A printed version is found in Shankar, *Treasury of Indian Tales*, 8-16.

Motifs include H508.1. King propounds questions to his sons

to determine successor; N332.7. Hidden fruit accidentally poisoned by snake.

O-sung and Han-um

There are many stories about these famous friends in Korea. I heard this from a Seoul high school student, In-Kyung Park, while visiting her class in 1996. A booklet of their tales was privately printed in 1978 at the renowned EWHA Women's University in Seoul, as part of a translation project by English students; it included a version of this tale written by Ji-moon Suh. Several other popular stories of the friends are included in Choi, *Korean Folktales*, 288.

Motifs include P319.7. Friendship without refusal; J120, Wisdom learned from children.

The Race

This version of a well-known theme was adapted from Hitam, *Folktales of Malaysia*. In Cambodia, the tale of popular Judge Rabbit and his race with the snails is very well known, found in Sau and others, *Cambodian Legends*, 18, and in classroom notes kindly supplied to me by Philip N. Jenner. Another variant from Indonesia is found in Asian Cultural Center for UNESCO, *Folk Tales from Asia for Children*, 3: 18-22.

Motifs include J1020. Strength in unity; K11.1. Race won by deception: relative helpers. Type 1074: Race won by deception: relative helpers.

CHAPTER 4: **Filial Piety and Respect for Elders**

Village of the Bell

This story is found in Choi, *Korean Folktales*, 165, where twelve variants are listed, and in Ha, *Folk Tales of Old Korea*, 88. I chose this variant for its age and for the images I could weave into it.

Motifs include N550. Unearthing hidden treasure; Q65. Filial duty rewarded.

The King Who Hated the Old

During a workshop in 1991 at Refugee Women's Alliance, Seattle, I told a Japanese version of this popular Asian story theme. Then Southeast Asian women shared variants they knew, including this one from Laos. Another version of this tale is found in Vongsakdy, *Folktales From Laos*, 25-27. A similar story from Japan is in Seki, ed., *Folktales of Japan*, 183-85. Thirty Japanese variants are listed in Yanagita, *Guide to the Japanese Folk Tale*, 168-69.

Motifs include J151.1. Wisdom of hidden old man saves kingdom. Type 981: Wisdom of hidden old man saves kingdom.

Bánh Dày, Bánh Chu'ng

This tale is widely known among Vietnamese Americans I have met; I heard it first from Emanuelle Chi Dang and others at Refugee Women's Alliance, Seattle, in 1990. Printed versions are gathered in *Viet-Su,* 9-31, and Le, *Popular Stories from Vietnam*, 1-2.

Motifs include H1574.3. King chosen by test; P17. Succession to the throne.

The Wild Pigeon

Yoriko Minami, a seventy-five-year-old storyteller and former teacher in Kanazawa, Japan, told me this in 1993. She said that her rather strict mother told it often to remind her to mind! Throughout East Asia, there are tales of unfilial animals, and of unfilial children who become birds with various cries. A close version is found in Mayer, ed., *Ancient Tales*, 272. Yanagita includes six pages of similar variants in *Guide to the Japanese Folk Tale*, 254-56, 268-70. A very popular Korean version tells of an unfilial green frog; in Choi, *Korean Folktales*, twelve variants of that type are listed.

Motifs include A2426.2. Cries of birds; D150. Transformation: man to bird.

CHAPTER 5: **Charity and Simplicity**

Kasa Jizo

There are countless versions in Japan of this well-loved story (Yanagita lists twenty variants). I heard this one from Toridamurisan, an elder legal advocate and singer in southern Kyushu island, as we shared stories informally in his crowded office, 1991. English versions are found in Mayer, ed., *Ancient Tales*, 87; in Uchida, *Sea of Gold*, 84-90; and Sakade, *Japanese Children's Favorite Stories*, 106-12.

Motifs include Q40. Kindness rewarded; W11. Generosity.

Kim Sondal and the River

The story presents one of Kim Sondal's best-known tricks. I heard this version in 1996 at an In-Pyo Children's Library in Pusan, Korea, from some charming children I met there. Korean variants in print include Pak, *Choseon Joenrae Donghwa-jib*, and Chul, *Pong Yi Kim Sondal Chun*, 31-58.

Motifs include J2300. Gullible fools; K282. Trickster sells what is not his to sell. Type 1539: Cleverness and gullibility.

Prince Vetsandon

When I began researching Southeast Asian tales to tell back to refugee families and their neighbors, I often heard this story mentioned. It is as popular among Buddhists as the famous *Ramayana* is among Hindus (see Cone and Gombrich, *Perfect Generosity*). There are even special days in several Southeast Asian countries devoted to sharing the story, and illustrations of it cover many temple walls.

I heard this version at a Cambodian temple in Seattle, 1990. Three monks there kindly chanted the story while poet Luoth Yin translated their words. The last of the *Jataka* tales (the Buddhist birth stories), it is found, under the more familiar Indian name *Prince Vessantara*, in Cowell, ed., *The Jataka* 6: 246-305, and in Cone and Gombrich, *Perfect Generosity*.

Motifs include V410. Charity rewarded; W11. Generosity.

Too Much

Stories travel in lovely ways; I heard this tale first in Japan from a friendly Filipino student, Linda Flores, studying in Sapporo. I later also found it in Mariano, *Folk Tales of the Philippines*, 120-23. A related version, also from the Philippines, shows lazy men turning into baboons (Sechrist, *Once in the First Times*, 37-38).

Motifs include A2238. Animal characteristics: punishment for greed; D118.2. Transformation man to monkey; Q280. Unkindness punished.

The Visit

My good friend Professor Rastogi in Delhi, India, told me this true anecdote soon after I arrived at his doorstop at 5 one morning in 1975, seeking shelter. I had met him only once before, briefly, in his Delhi office, but when my housing plans suddenly changed and I arrived penniless (and rupeeless) at his door, he and his family immediately took me in and showed me the best of Indian hospitality.

CHAPTER 6: **Hard Work and Study**

References

1. Arthur Ryder, trans., *The Panchatantra* (Chicago: University of Chicago Press, 1964), 442.

Ondal the Fool

This story is known by many in Korea; it was first recorded in the old Korean book of history, *Annals of the Three Kingdoms*. It has recently been shared in a lovely picturebook version (Ree, *Princess*

Pyongkang and Ondal the Fool) and in Ha, *Folk Tales of Old Korea.*

Motifs include T121.3.1. Princess marries lowly man; T97. Father opposed to daughter's marriage; W32. Bravery.

Dividing the Property

Several teachers shared versions of this well-known tale at a workshop in Dhaka, Bangladesh, 1993. They told me that in some versions it is two elder women who divide the property. The story is found in Chaudhury, *Folk Tales of Bangladesh*, and in Jasimuddin, *Folk Tales of Bangladesh*, 20-25.

Motifs include J242.8. In dividing property, clever brother takes best parts. Type 1030: The crop division.

A Clever Trade

Prakash Jain, a journalist and friend, told me this during my first trip to India in 1970. In some versions, not only is the Goddess Lakshmi invited in, but the Goddess of Poverty or a similar figure of gloom leaves the house, promising never to return. Madhur Jaffrey retells that version in *Seasons of Splendour*; a South Indian version is told in Gupte, *Hindu Holidays*; and one set in North India is in Shankar, *Treasury of Indian Tales*, 69-76.

Motifs include W216.1. Thrifty merchant tells son even a snake laid by will be useful; Q86. Reward for industry.

The Wise Merchant

During a storytelling workshop in 1993, I heard a short version of this tale in Karachi, Pakistan, from a young teacher at the exciting Teachers' Resource Centre there. It is also found in Khan, *Folktales from Sindh*, 98-101.

The tale's wisdom about wasting is repeated often in South Asia. Once, while walking down the street in New York City with a visiting Indian teacher, I saw her close to tears when she noticed all the usable things piled up as garbage on the streets. We spent hours trying in vain to find a way of shipping some back to her school.

Motifs include J10. Wisdom acquired from experience; W131.1. Profligate wastes entire fortune before beginning his own adventures.

CHAPTER 7: **Nature and Humans**

References

1. Shigeru Kayano, *Our Land was a Forest*, trans. by Kyoko Selden and Lily Selden (Boulder, Colo.: Westview, 1994), 19.

2. Hong-key Yoon, *Geomantic Relationships Between Culture and Nature in Korea*, Asian Folklife and Social Life Monographs, vol. 89 (Taipei, 1976), 1.

The Scratch

This is another simple teaching tale I heard from Ram Swarup in India. It can be found in an extended version in Ramakrishna, *Sri Ramakrishna Tells Stories*, 3-6. The same message, clothed in a different story, is found in DeSpain, *Eleven Nature Tales*, 13-16.

Motifs include A401. Mother Earth conceived as mother of all things.

A Girl, A Horse

In 1991, I attended an incredible storytellers' retreat at an old Japanese hot springs inn nestled amidst northern mountains. One night, dressed in traditional farmer's dress and speaking in her local dialect, seventy-seven-year-old Metokisan quietly told this tale, recalling the warmth and closeness she felt when her grandmother shared it at bedtime. Weeks later, I heard another version in Tono, a northern town rich in folklore, when I visited a *magariya*, the oldstyle house where rooms were indeed kept for valued horses. Versions in print include Yanagita, *Legends of Tono*, 49-50, and two collected tales from Nagano and Yamanashi in Yanagita, *Guide to the Japanese Folk Tale*, 312.

Motifs include B611.3. Horse paramour; W34. Loyalty.

The Right Site

My Korean friend's father had an auspicious grave: a traditional grass-covered mound, high on a mountain, overlooking a valley. After I saw it, I found this little anecdote in Yoon, *Geomantic Relationships*, 148. It is also in Choi, *Korean Folktales*, 147, where three versions are listed. Two related Chinese tales about geomancy can be found in Eberhardt, ed., *Folktales of China*, 69-72.

Motifs include N134. Persons effect change of luck; E754.3. Burial in certain ground assures going to heaven.

The Children

This poignant tale of abandoned children is well known among the Lao immigrants I have met. Several women at Refugee Women's Alliance have told it to me, as well as a neighbor, Somephone Phommahaxay, who shared it with me in 1991 in her Seattle home. There is a written version found in Vongsakdy, *Folktales From Laos*, 62. A similar story from the Philippines in Sechrist (*Once in the First*

Times, 37-38) has lazy men turned into baboons.

Motifs include A1861. Creation of monkey; A2260. Animal characteristics from transformation; S321. Destitute parents abandon children.

CHAPTER 8: **Faith and Belief**

God in All

This is a favorite story of the beloved and popular saint and sage Sri Ramakrishna of India (1836-1886). There are several active Ramakrishna Missions in India today which offer sermons and stories along with medical and social services. This tale I heard during an evening lecture, in 1980, at their Mission in Chennai.

The story is also found in Ramakrishna, *Tales and Parables*, 201-02. Very similar tales are told about the South Indian sage Avvaiar (Rajagopalachari, *Avvaiar: the Great Tamil Poetess*, 6) and in the Sufi tradition (Khan, *Tales*, 92-93).

Motifs include J153. Wisdom from holy man; V510. Religious visions.

A Final Lesson

Emanuelle Chi Dang, who came to Seattle as a refugee, was proud of her father's learning and his position as a respected official in old Vietnam. In 1994, while we ate a delicious Vietnamese lunch in Seattle, she told me this little anecdote from her father. It can also be found in Binh, *Short Stories of Vietnam and China*, and in Van Over, ed., *Taoist Tales*, 195.

Motifs include J153. Wisdom from holy man.

A Good Beating

I had the great fortune to spend ten months exchanging English lessons through poetry and song for Tibetan dance lessons at the Tibetan School of Dance and Drama in Dharamsala, India in 1975. When we gathered for meals outside, staring up at the mighty Himalayas, stories were often shared: true and sad stories of escape from Tibet when the Chinese took over, tales of tricksters, and stories of mystics and monks. I heard this tale in one of those sessions. Later I also found versions in Das, *The Snow Lion's Turquoise Mane*, 67, and in Chopel, *Folk Tales of Tibet*, 69-71.

Motifs include N848. Saint as helper; Q272. Greed punished.

Salmaan al-Faarsi

I found the inspiring story of Salmaan when browsing in a

bookstore in Karachi, Pakistan. His life is related in Murad, *The Long Search*, and in Sieny, *Muslim Heroes*, 4: 66-71, a fine source of biographies and legends.

Motifs include V461. Clerical virtue; V461.8. Poverty as saintly virtue.

Kirihataji

"I know why he died smiling," said my friend's mother when her husband passed away in Osaka. "Three times in our lives we were pilgrims on that sacred route with Kobo Daishi, going around that island to visit each temple. I know that's why he was blessed with such a good death." Stories about Kobo Daishi and his good deeds are found everywhere on the island of Shikoku. I was happy to visit several of the temples in 1991 and heard this legend then from a fellow traveler. One variant is found in Statler, *Japanese Pilgrimage*, 46-47, and a related version is in Mayer, ed., *Ancient Tales*, 87. For more on Kobo Daishi, try Hakeda, trans., *Kukai: Major Works*.

Motifs include A 483.1. Goddess of mercy, Kwan Yin; V220. Saints; V411. Miraculous reward for charities; V112. Temples; V127. Image of deity in wood.

Valli and Kande Yaka

I met Patrick Harrigan first on the Internet and later in Chennai, India, 1997. He started to study the Kataragama jungle shrine in 1971, and has heard many versions of this tale since in his research. From 1989 he has been the acting editor of the Kataragama Research and Publications Project. He writes: "The story of Valli Amma's romance with the god of Kataragama Peak has circulated throughout Sri Lanka and South India for at least 2,000 years. It is an oral tradition that is told in many versions and several languages including Sinhala, Tamil, and the language of the Vaddas, the forest-dwelling hunting people of Sri Lanka. The story—which may be legend or may be proto-history—relates an extraordinary incident that left a lasting impression upon the neolithic hunting and gathering people whom it describes."

Motifs include A188. Gods in love with humans; K1811. Gods in disguise visit mortals.

CHAPTER 9: **Fantasy and the Supernatural**

Zhuang Brocade

This lovely tale comes from the Zhuang people of China, a large minority group numbering over 17 million and living in the Southeastern region of China. I adapted it from versions in *Peacock*

Maiden, 54-67, and in Van Over, ed., *Taoist Tales*, 45-51. For a recent picturebook version, see Demi, *The Magic Tapestry*.

Motifs include D454.3. Transformation: cloth to other object; H1242. Youngest brother alone succeeds on quest; N825.3. Old woman helper.

Three Charms

When I surveyed over two hundred Japanese storytellers, by mail and in person, in 1991, this tale was picked most often as a favorite. The phrase at the end of the story, "Gochisosama deshita" is usually said at the end of a meal, as a sigh of satisfaction and a thank you.

I heard the tale in several storyswap sessions in Japan. One version is found on a kamishibai as *Taberareta Yamanba* by Miyoko Matsutani, (Tokyo: Doshinsha). Thirteen variants are listed in Yanagita, *Guide to the Japanese Folk Tale*, 100, and it is also found in Seki, ed., *Folktales of Japan*, 47-50.

Motifs include D672. Obstacle Flight; D1611. Magic object answers for fugitive. Type 313H: Magic flight from witch.

The Woodcutter and the Bird

This well-known tale echoes themes from two of the most popular tales in the p'ansori storytelling repertoire: *Heungbu Nolbu*, about a sparrow's gratitude, and *Sim Ch'ong*, which tells of a daughter's sacrifice for her father.

I heard versions of this several times: from Laura Simms in a workshop years ago, and from Korean friends both in 1995 and 1996. There are sixteen variants listed in Choi, *Korean Folktales*, 40. An older retelling in English is in Jewett, *Which was Witch*, 59-64, and a recent retelling for middle school is found in Petersen, "Thirst for Knowledge," in flora Joy, ed., *Exploring Cultures and Their Stories*, 43-46.

Motifs include B365.0.1. Bird grateful for rescue of its young; E234.3. Return from dead to avenge death; W28. Self-sacrifice.

CHAPTER 10: **National Identity and Pride**

References

1. Bernard Reines, *A People's Hero* (New York: Praeger Publishers, 1971), 180.

Silent Debate

This tale was told, in 1996, at an inspiring meeting in Seoul,

Korea, of the Comparative Folklore Society with members from Japan, Korea, and China. Professor Suh, a natural storyteller, shared it as part of his lecture. I later found it in Choi, *Korean Folktales*, 280, where nine variants are listed from Korea. A well-known version in Jewish tradition can be seen in Dorson, ed., *Folk Tales Told Around the World*, 169.

Motifs include J1804. Conversation by sign language mutually misunderstood. Type 924: Sign language misunderstood.

Phù Dổ'ng Thiên Vư'o'ng

This well-known hero story I heard at Refugee Women's Alliance, Seattle, from Emanuelle Chi Dang and her friend, Laihung. They spent time as well giving me authentic details and images to include, for they were eager to have Americans learn about Vietnamese heroes. A shortened version, in four languages, is found in *Viet-Su*, 33-63.

Motifs include A526.7. Culture hero performs remarkable feats of strength and skill.

A Chey

Thnenh (or Thmenh) Chey, more popularly called A Chey, is a beloved trickster in Cambodia and in the Cambodian American community. He is a young boy who always seems to get in and out of trouble. I heard many of his tales from Putha Touch, Lina Mao Wall, and also from Cambodian newcomers at Refugee Women's Alliance in Seattle. A version of this story is written, along with other tricks, in a French article given me by Putha: "Thmenh Chey" from *Contes Khmer*, 51-97 (n.p., n.d.).

Motifs include H509.5. Test: telling skillful lie; J1675. Clever dealing with a king. Type 1542A: Return for tools.

The Zither-Met Friends

Kate Stevens writes: "The story began around 300 C.E. in *Lie Zi* [Graham, trans., 119-20], in a deceptively simple form. Many years later, this Beijing Drumsong version is one of several versions still current. Beijing Drumsongs are marvellously compact, moving tales, sung in a space of 20-25 minutes. Actually, *Zither-Met Friends* ends with the banquet, then refers to the zither smashing scene, since a Chinese audience would know all of the story. I add that last section for audiences here, from another, less common Drumsong, *Yu Boya Smashes the Zither*.

I hope you will look up a good recording of the *guqin (ku ch'in)*; the quiet, subdued music repays careful listening ... The beginning music is as sung by Zhang Cuifeng, about 1958, and my prose version is adapted from her text. If you wish to say the beginning lines, I suggest you consult Siu Wang-Ngai's *Chinese Opera* for its fine pronounciation key, since it is too difficult to cover here."

Motifs include H503. Test of musical ability; P311. Sworn brethren; P428. Musician.

José Rizal

When I asked friends from the Philippines whom to include in this chapter, the name of José Rizal always came up first. I went to the Internet, where a number of sites on Rizal can be found, and also located two fine books that I used as sources: Zaide and Zaide, *Rizal and Other Great Filipinos*, and Reines, *A People's Hero*.

CHAPTER 11: **Wit and Wisdom**

References

1. Shigeru Kayano, *Our Land was a Forest*, trans. by Kyoko Selden and Lily Selden (Boulder, Colo.: Westview, 1994), 125.

Andare

Andare is very popular in Sri Lanka, as I learned in Colombo. After I told stories of American tricksters at the American Center there, several guests came up and shared Andare tales, including this one, at the reception. The story is also found in Feinberg, ed., *Asian Laughter*, 548, and in Ratnapala, *Folklore of Sri Lanka*, 9.

Motifs include J2300. Gullible fools. Type 1539: Tricksters and their victims.

Xieng Mieng

The Lao women at Refugee Women's Alliance in Seattle loved to share stories of Xieng Mieng, and this one was a favorite told by many. It is found, with several other Xieng Mieng tales, in Kaignavongsa and Fincher, *Legends of the Lao*. An interesting variant, from Afghanistan, is found in Yolen, ed., *Favorite Folktales*, 413.

Motifs include H1182.2. King asks for new trick; Q91. Cleverness rewarded.

Hodja

My good friend, artist Sultan Ali, used to tell some of Hodja's tricks, including this one, while we talked in his home at Cholamandal, India. The historical Hodja probably lived in thirteenth-century Turkey, but his wit is now enjoyed worldwide. For more tricks, see Dorson, ed., *Folk Tales Told Around the World*, 137;

Yolen, ed., *Favorite Folktales*, 173; and Walker, *Watermelons, Walnuts and the Wisdom of Allah.*

Motifs include K18. Throwing contest won by deception; L400. Pride brought low.

Si Kabayan

In 1993, while giving a workshop for the University of Washington on Southeast Asian Storytelling, I was rather nervous to find a visiting professor from Indonesia in the audience. But when I shared a few tales of a favorite West Javanese trickster, Si Kabayan, she began to beam. After the workshop she came up and thanked me for sharing her culture and then we sat over tea as she told me this joke. For another Kabayan tale, see *Laughing Together*, 55-58.

Motifs include J2198. Bewailing a calamity that had not occurred.

Ainu Wit

This small piece comes from Kayano's memoir, *Our Land Was a Forest*, and is a lovely example of the wit of a people who treasured eloquence and speaking well. The Ainu scholar mentioned, Kyosuke Kindaichi, whom author Kayano respected and worked with, did much to preserve Ainu language.

The Sky is Dark, is Dark

Professor Jeff Tsay, whom I found online, was most helpful and eager to share his homeland. He in turn located a student, Joanna C. Yu, who volunteered to translate several popular Taiwanese folk songs. This light-hearted farmers' song, which Jeff remembers everyone singing when he was young, is one of her fine efforts.

Endless Tale

Just as Japan has a rich store of onomatopoeia, it also has a wealth of endless tales. I heard this one from my friend Ritsuko Hosakawa on Noto Peninsula in Japan. She told several such tales as she showed me her marvelous handmade books. Yanagita lists sixteen types of endless tales in *Guide to the Japanese Folk Tale*, 315-16, and a similar version is included in Yolen, ed., *Favorite Folktales*, 45.

Motifs include Z11. Endless tales.

The Ceremony

My husband, Paramasivam, never forgot the meaning of "baby shower" after this experience. Our cross-cultural marriage is rich in such discoveries, as we exchange different stories, words, and proverbs, and sometimes argue over different values!

A Costly Smell

This tale is a Burmese version of a very popular theme in judgement lore. I adapted this from Aung, *Folk Tales of Burma*, 72, because I was intrigued with Princess Learned-in-the-Law. A Cambodian version is found in Carpenter, *The Elephant's Bathtub*, 100-07. Yolen includes a variant from Africa in *Favorite Folktales* 406-07. For more on Park Moon Su, see Zong's *Folk Tales from Korea*, 54-55; and for tales of Judge Ooka, try Edmond's *The Case of the Marble Monster*.

Motifs include J 1172.2. Clink of money for smell of food. Type 926C: Wise Judges.

A Woman's Wit

I enjoyed this tale of a clever woman and so retold it from two versions found in Vaidya, *Folk Tales of Nepal*, 99-112, and in Sakya and Griffith, *Tales of Kathmandu*, 188-91.

Motifs include G512.3. Ogre burned to death; G450. Falling into ogre's power—misc.

Momma, the Little Crab is Snapping my Finger

This funny teaching tale comes from Tossa and MacDonald, *Folktales and Storytelling*, 19, and is told by student tellers in Thailand. It is reprinted courtesy of the authors. Dr. Tossa is working on further translations of Isan epics and stories, and she continues to guide storytellers in her area.

Motifs include W116.7. Use of strange language to show education; W165. False pride.

Amazing Indian Trains

This joke is one of many I heard from Maya Thiagarajan in Chennai, in 1994. She heard it in her school there, as she did many jokes. Maya was then in tenth grade and an endless source of jokes.

Motifs include J1800. One thing mistaken for another—misc. Type 1349: Fools, misc.

Chasing the Monkeys

In 1997, while hunting online for photographs to use in a book of South Indian stories, I found A.D. Edward Raj, a most helpful researcher at the ISRO Satellite Centre in Bangalore, India. I then met him in South India, and spent part of the Christmas holiday with his lovely family. Months later, I wrote of my search for jokes, and he immediately sent back two favorites that are widely told in his office. This one I especially enjoyed, and share through his kindness.

Motifs include J1160. Clever pleading; Q91. Cleverness rewarded.

Works Cited

Alvares, Claude. "The Genius of Hindu Civilization." *Illustrated Weekly of India*, June 15, 1986, 9-16.

Aarne, Antti, and Stith Thompson. *The Types of the Folktale*. Helsinki: Suomalainen Tiedeakatemia, 1961.

Asian Cultural Center for UNESCO. *Folk Tales from Asia for Children Everywhere*. Book 3. New York: Weatherhill, 1976.

Aung, Maung Htin. *Folk Tales of Burma*. New Delhi: Sterling, 1976.

Binh, Truong Van. *Thirty Best Short Stories of Vietnam and China*. Houston: Zieleks, n.d.

Carpenter, Frances. *The Elephant's Bathtub*. Garden City: Doubleday, 1962.

Chaudhury, P.C. Roy. *Folk Tales of Bangladesh*. New Delhi: Sterling, 1990.

Choi, In-hak. *A Type Index of Korean Folktales*. Seoul: Myongji University, 1978.

Chopel, Norbu. *Folk Tales of Tibet*. Dharamsala, India: Library of Tibetan Works and Archives, 1984.

Chul, Shin Sang. *Pong Yi Kim Sondal Chun*. Seoul: Yoon Chin Moon Hwa, 1994.

Cone, Margaret, and R. Gombrich, trans. *The Perfect Generosity of Prince Vessantara*. Oxford: Clarendon Press, 1977.

Cowell, E.B., ed. *The Jataka*. 6 vols. London: Pali Text Society, 1967.

Das, K.B., and L.K. Mahapatra. *Folklore of Orissa*. New Delhi: National Book Trust, 1979.

Das, Surya. *The Snow Lion's Turquoise Mane*. San Francisco: HarperCollins, 1992.

Demi. *The Magic Tapestry*. New York: Holt, 1994.

DeSpain, Pleasant. *Eleven Nature Tales*. Little Rock: August House, 1996.

Dharampal. *Indian Science and Technology in the Eighteenth Century*. Delhi: Impex India, 1971.

Dorson, Richard, ed. *Folktales Told Around the World*. Chicago: University of Chicago Press, 1975.

Eberhardt, Wolfram, ed. *Folktales of China*. New York: Washington Square Press, 1973.

Edmonds, I.G. *The Case of the Marble Monster*. New York: Scholastic, 1961.

Feinberg, Leonard, ed. *Asian Laughter*. New York: Weatherhill, 1971.

Graham, A.C., trans. *The Book of Lieh-tzu*. London: John Murrary, 1960.

Gupte, Raj Bahadur. *Hindu Holidays and Ceremonials*. Calcutta: Thacker, Spink & Co, 1919.
Ha, Tae-hung. *Folk Tales of Old Korea*. Seoul: Yonsei University Press, 1958.
__________. *Tales from the Three Kingdoms*. Seoul: Yonsei University Press, 1984.
Hakeda, Yoshito S., trans. *Kukai: Major Works*. New York: Columbia University Press, 1972.
Hitam, Zakaria bin. *Folk Tales of Malaysia*. New Delhi: Sterling, 1986.
Jaffrey, Madhur. *Seasons of Splendour*. New York: Atheneum, 1985.
Jasimuddin. *Folk Tales of Bangladesh*. Translated by C. Painter and H. Jasimuddin. Dacca: Oxford University Press, 1974.
Jewett, Eleanore. *Which Was Witch?* New York: Viking, 1959.
Kaignavongsa, Xay, and Hugh Fincher. *Legends of the Lao*. Bangkok: Geodata System, 1993.
Kayano, Shigeru. *Our Land was a Forest*. Translated by Kyoko Selden and Lily Selden. Boulder, Colo.: Westview, 1994.
Khan, Hazrat Inayat. *Tales*. New Lebanon, New York: Sufi Order Publications, 1980.
Khan, Shereen, trans. *Folktales from Sindh*. Islamabad: Academy of Letters, 1990.
Kim, Woo Ok. "P'ansori: An Indigenous Theater of Korea." Ph.D. diss., New York University, 1980.
Kyi, Aung San Suu. *Freedom From Fear*. New York: Viking Penguin, 1991.
Laughing Together. Delhi: National Book Trust, 1991.
Le, Tinh Thong. *Popular Stories from Vietnam*. San Diego: Institute for Cultural Pluralism, n.d.
MacDonald, Margaret Read. *The Storyteller's Sourcebook*. Detroit: Neal-Schuman/Gale Research, 1982.
Mariano, M. *Folk Tales of the Philippines*. New Delhi: Sterling, 1982.
Matsutani, Miyoko. *Taberareta Yamanba*. Tokyo: Doshinsha, 1990.
______________. *Yamanba no Fushiki*. Tokyo: Popurasha, 1967, and in English as *The Witch's Magic Cloth* by Lothrop, Lee & Shepard, 1983.
Mayer, Fanny Hagin, ed. *Ancient Tales in Modern Japan*. Bloomington: Indiana University Press, 1984.
Murad, Khumman. *The Long Search*. Leicester, U.K.: The Islamic Foundation, 1990.
Naisbitt, John. *Megatrends Asia*. New York: Simon & Schuster, 1996.
Pak, Yeong-man. *Choseon Joenrae Donghwa-jib*. Seoul: Hagyesa, 1940.
Peacock Maiden. Beijing: Foreign Languages Press, 1981.

Petersen, Roger. "A Thirst for Knowledge." In *Exploring Cultures and Their Stories*, edited by Flora Joy, 37-52. Torrance, Cal.: Frank Schaffer, 1996.
Peterson, Sally. "Translating Experience and the Reading of a Story Cloth." *Journal of American Folklore* 101 (Jan.-Mar. 1998): 6-22.
Pihl, Marshall. *The Korean Singer of Tales*. Cambridge: Harvard University Press, 1994.
Rajagopalachari, C. *Avvaiar, The Great Tamil Poetess*. Bombay: Bharatiya Vidya Bhavan, 1971.
Ramakrishna. *Sri Ramakrishna Tells Stories*. Madras: Sri Ramakrishna Math, 1986.
Ramakrishna. *Tales and Parables of Sri Ramakrishna*. Madras: Sri Ramakrishna Math, 1947.
Ramanujan, A.K. ed. *Folktales from India*. New York: Pantheon, 1991.
Ratnapala, Nandasena. *Folklore of Sri Lanka*. Colombo: State Printing Corporation, 1991.
Ree, Young-ho. *Princess Pyongkang and Ondal the Fool*. Seoul: Daihak, 1982.
Reines, Bernard. *A People's Hero*. New York: Praeger Publishers, 1971.
Ryder, Arthur, trans. *The Panchatantra*. Chicago: University of Chicago Press, 1964.
Sakade, Florence. *Japanese Children's Favorite Stories*. Rutland, Vt.: Charles Tuttle, 1958.
Sakya, Karna, and Linda Griffith. *Tales of Kathmandu*. Kathmandu: Mandala Book Point, 1992.
Satyarthi, Devendra. *Meet My People*. Hyderabad: Chetana Prakashan, 1951.
Sau, Chandha, Bettie Lou Sechrist, and Kry Lay, eds. *Cambodian Legends*. Long Beach: South East Asian Learners Project, 1978.
Sechrist, Elizabeth. *Once in the First Times: Folk Tales From the Philippines*. Philadelphia: Macrae Smith, 1969.
Seki, Keigo, ed. *Folktales of Japan*. Chicago: University of Chicago Press, 1963.
Shankar. *Treasury of Indian Tales*. New Delhi: Children's Book Trust, 1967.
Sieny, Maumoud Esmail. *Muslim Heroes*. Book 4. Karachi: International Islamic Publishers Ltd., 1989.
Song, Bang-song. "Kwangdae Ka: A Source Material for the P'ansori Tradition." *Korea Journal* 6 (Aug. 1976): 24-32.
Statler, Oliver. *Japanese Pilgrimage*. New York: Morrow, 1983.
Stevens, Catherine (Kate). "Peking (Beijing) Drumsinging." Ph.D. diss., Harvard University, 1972.

Stevens, Kate. "The World of the Chinese Storyteller." *Appleseed Quarterly* 7 (Spring 1997): 17-23.

Thompson, Stith. *Motif-Index of Folk Literature.* Bloomington: Indiana University Press, 1955-58.

Thurlow, Clifford. *Stories from Beyond the Clouds.* Dharamsala, India: Library of Tibetan Works and Archives, 1981.

Tossa, Wajuppa, and Margaret Read MacDonald. *Folktales and Storytelling.* Mahasarakham, Thailand: Mahasarakham Storytelling Project, 1996.

Uchida, Yoshiko. *The Sea of Gold.* New York: Charles Scribner's Sons, 1965.

Vaidya, Karunakar. *Folk Tales of Nepal.* Kathmandu: Ratna Pustak Bhandar, 1979.

Van Over, Raymond, ed. *Taoist Tales.* New York: Mentor, 1973.

Vang, Lue, and Judy Lewis. *Grandmother's Path, Grandfather's Way: Hmong Preservation Project.* San Francisco: Zellerbach Family Fund, 1984.

Viet-Su Bang Tranh. Ontario, Canada: Que Huong, n.d.

Vongsakdy, Somsy. *Folktales From Laos.* Seattle: Seattle Public Schools, 1982.

Walker, Barbara. *Watermelons, Walnuts, and the Wisdom of Allah.* New York: Parents' Magazine Press, 1967.

Yanagita, Kunio. *The Legends of Tono.* Translated by Ronald A. Morse. Tokyo: The Japan Foundation, 1975.

____________. *The Yanagita Kunio Guide to the Japanese Folk Tale.* Translated by Fanny Hagin Mayer. Bloomington: Indiana University Press, 1986.

Yolen, Jane, ed. *Favorite Folktales from Around the World.* New York: Pantheon, 1986.

Yoon, Hong-key. *Geomantic Relationships Between Culture and Nature in Korea.* Asian Folklore and Social Life Monographs, vol. 89. Taipei, 1976.

Zaide, Gregorio, and Sonia Zaide. *Rizal and Other Great Filipinos.* Manila: National Book Store, 1987.

GLOSSARY

The glossary contains terms pertaining especially to storytelling styles or important cultural details. Please note that the spelling of many foreign words is often done in several different styles of transcription; thus many of the entries may be seen elsewhere in slightly different forms.

Beijing Drumsinging: One of many Chinese storytelling styles, this uses skilled telling with musical accompaniment.

bhagavatar: A storyteller in Harikatha style popular in South India.

bunko: Japanese home library of neighborhood children, either in actual home or in local center; often features storytelling.

burra katha: Form of three-person storytelling famous is state of Andhra Pradesh, South India.

Chakyar kuttu: Sophisticated, older Indian storytelling form, performed in temples of Kerala state by member of *Chakyar* community.

Ganesh: Popular elephant-headed god in India; remover of obstacles.

guru: Teacher in Indian society; traditionally used oral instruction to pass on learning in religion and art.

Hajj: Pilgrimage to Makkah, to be done at least once in the life of a Muslim, if possible.

Harikatha: Form of storytelling now especially strong in parts of South India; very sophisticated, using much music and improvisation.

irori: Firepit in traditional Japanese homes; often the center for storytelling during long, cold nights.

Jizo: A Buddhist deity, now identified as a *kami* in Japan and found often as a statue. Koyasu Jizo is protector of children.

kami: A Japanese deity, of which there are many kinds.

kamishibai: "Paper theater"; form of Japanese storytelling using pictures in sequence. (A similar Indian form, using painted picture scenes, is called *chitra katha*.)

Kannon: Buddhist deity found in East Asia, usually given feminine attributes, and one that appears in dreams.

kathaprasangam: Musical storytelling in Kerala, without religious messages of themes.

kavad: Special prop used in parts of northwestern India, with story scenes painted on panels that unfold to tell tales.

kodan: Older, classical style of recitation/telling in Japan; not so popular today as it once was.

kolam or rangoli: Intricate drawing on street or floor, used for greeting, ritual, and/or celebration; known by various regional names across India.

mudras: Elegant hand sign language used in classical Indian dance and in ottan thullal storytelling.

Mukashi, mukashi: Common story beginning in Japan, meaning "long, long ago."

Oshimai: Short form of a traditional ending in Japanese. Another common one showing a happy ending is *medetashi*.

ottan thullal: Storytelling form from Kerala state, South India, with costume, dance, satire, and music.

p'ansori: Korean operatic storytelling style, with one teller and drummer. The basic p'ansori repertoire consists today of five popular pieces.

Parvati: Form of the goddess in Hinduism; consort to Lord Siva.

patas: Vertical scrolls used to tell stories in northeastern India. Wandering tellers who use them are called *patuas*.

phad: Storytelling scroll used in Rajasthan, North India, to tell tales, usually of heroes Pabuji or Devanarayana.

rakshasa: A demon character in Hindu thought and lore.

raga: Melodic structure used in Indian music, expressing a mood. Certain ragas are used frequently in various Indian storytelling styles.

rakugo: Japanese storytelling, often comic, performed in yose theaters, by very skilled tellers (*hanashika*).

Rama: Hero of the epic *Ramayana*, known for his keeping of dharma (duty); incarnation of Vishnu.

Siva: Popular god in Indian thought with role of destroyer. He dwells on Mt. Kailash and is known for his cosmic dance.

tala: Beats or rhythmic cycles used in Indian music and storytelling.

tanka: Elaborately illustrated scrolls of Tibetans, showing pictures of deities for ritual, or stories to be shared.

villu pattu: Storytelling form in southern tip of India, with large musical bow played by main teller, accompanied by others.

yamanba: Japanese creature that can change shapes and lives in mountains. (A few other important Japanese story creatures include *tengu*, with a long nose and wings; *kappa*, with saucer-shaped headtop; *oni*, with horns and a fierce look; *tanuki*, raccoonlike trickster; and *kitsune*, fox trickster.)

yukura: Epic changed by Ainu minority in Japan, telling of their gods and goddesses.

Further Resources

Here, first, is a sampling of helpful books on Asian storytelling. (The list of works on Asia, past and present, would fill another entire volume.) For more reading suggestions, please contact the resource centers and Internet sites noted later in this section.

Beck, Brenda, and others, eds. *Folktales of India*. Chicago: University of Chicago Press, 1987.

Blackburn, Stuart H. *Singing of Birth and Death: Texts in Performance*. Philadelphia: University of Pennsylvania Press, 1988.

Carrison, Muriel Paskin. *Cambodian Folk Stories*. Rutland, Vt.: Charles E. Tuttle, 1987.

Chin, Yin-lien, Yetta Center, and Mildred Ross. *Traditional Chinese Folktales*. Armonk, NY: M.E. Sharpe, 1989.

Chun, Shin-yong, ed. *Korean Folk Tales*. Seoul: Si-sa-yong-o-sa, 1982.

Dorson, Richard. *Folk Legends of Japan*. Rutland, Vt.: Charles E. Tuttle, 1981.

Dorson, Richard, gen. ed. *Folk Tales of the World* Series. Bloomington: Indiana University Press. (Includes several fine volumes on individual Asian countries.)

Duong, Van Quyen. *Beyond the East Wind: Legends and Folktales of Vietnam*. Thousand Oaks, Cal.: Burn, Hart, 1976.

Gurumurthy, Preemila. *Kathakalaksepa*. Madras: International Society for the Investigation of Ancient Civilizations, 1994.

Ha, Tae-Hung. *Korean Nights Entertainment*. Seoul: Yonsei University, 1969.

Hart, Donn V. *Riddles in Filipino Folklore*. Syracuse, N.Y.: Syracuse University Press, 1964.

Han, Suzanne Crowder. *Korean Folk and Fairy Tales*. Elizabeth, N.J.: Hollym, 1991.

Khorana, Meena. *The Indian Subcontinent in Literature for Children and Young Adults: An Annotated Bibliography of English Language Books*. Westport, Conn.: Greenwood Press, 1991.

Mair, Victor H. *Painting and Performance*. Honolulu: University of Hawaii Press, 1988.

Morioka, Heinz, and Miyoko Sasaki. *Rakugo, the Popular Narrative Art of Japan*. Cambridge: Council on East Asian Studies at Harvard, 1990.

Narayan, Kirin. *Storytellers, Saints, and Scoundrels*. Philadelphia: University of Pennsylvania Press, 1989.

Pellowski, Anne. *The World of Storytelling: A Practical Guide to the Origins, Development, and Applications of Storytelling*. Rev. ed. Bronx, N.Y.: Wilson, 1990.

Richman, Paula, ed. *Many Ramayanas: The Diversity of a Narrative Tradition in South Asia*. Berkeley: University of California Press, 1991.

Sen Gupta, Sankar. *The Patas and the Patuas of Bengal*. Calcutta: Indian Publications, 1973.

Shaikh, Munir. *Teaching About Islam and Muslims*. Fountain Valley, Cal.: Council on Islamic Education, 1995.

Stevens, Kate. *Long Life Village: Chinese Clappertales*. Victoria, B.C.: Sand Gull Press, 1997. Available from Kate Stevens, 2115 Lorne Terrace, Victoria, B.C., Canada V8S 2H9.

Terada, Alice M. *Under the Starfruit Tree: Folktales from Vietnam*. Honolulu: University of Hawaii Press, 1989.

Wheeler, Post. *Tales from the Japanese Storytellers*. Rutland, Vt.: Tuttle, 1976.

World Folklore Series from Libraries Unlimited, Colo. Excellent series featuring several volumes of story collections with cultural material on selected Asian countries.

Zong, In-sob. *Folk Tales from Korea*. Elizabeth, N.J.: Hollym, 1982.

Publishers and Resource Centers

AmicaInternational
1201 1st Avenue South
Suite 304
Seattle, WA 98134
Ph: 206-467-1035
Fax: 206-467-1522
E-mail: AMICA@ix.netcom.com
Internet: http://www.islamicpublishers.com
Books, cards, children's magazine, calendar with Muslim holidays

Apsara Media for Intercultural Education
13659 Victory Blvd., Suite 577
Van Nuys, CA 91401
Ph: 818-785-1498
Fax: 818-785-1495
Materials on South and Southeast Asian arts

Asia for Kids
P.O. Box 9096
Cincinnati, OH 45209-0096
Ph: 800-765-5885
Fax: 513-271-8856
Asian books, toys, crafts

Asia Society
725 Park Avenue
New York, NY 10021
AskAsia Ph: 888-ASK-ASIA
AskAsia Fax: 888-FAX-ASIA
URL: http://www.askasia.org
Asian Educational Resource Center, with publications and information about Asia through AskAsia help

Brigham Young University
D.M. Kennedy Center for International Studies
Publication Services
280 HRCB
Provo, UT 84602
Publishes Culturgrams: concise, useful country notes

Cellar Book Shop
18090 Wyoming
Detroit, MI 48221
Books on and from Southeast Asia

Cheng & Tsui Company
25 West Street
Boston, MA 02111
Ph: 617-426-6074
Fax: 617-426-3669
Royal Asiatic Society publications and other materials on Asia

Heritage Key
6102 East Mescal Street
Scottsdale, AZ 85254-5419
Ph: 602-483-3313
Fax: 602-483-9666
Asian books, dolls, games

Kamishibai for Kids
P.O. Box 20069
Park West Station
N.Y., N.Y. 10025-1510
Ph / Fax: 212-662-5836
Kamishibai sets for sale

KAZI Publications
3023-27 W. Belmont Ave.
Chicago, IL 60618
Ph: 773-267-7001
Fax: 773-267-7002
E-mail: Kazibooks@kazi.org
URL: http://www.kazi.org
Materials on Islam and the Muslim world

Pacific Rim Publications
Box 5204, Station B
Victoria, BC V8R6N4
Materials on Asian Pacific Rim

Shen's Books and Supplies
8625 Hubbard Road
Auburn, CA 95602-7815
Ph: 800-456-6660
Fax: 530-888-6763
URL: http://www.shens.com
E-mail: info@shens.com
Multicultural catalog

South Asia Books
P.O. Box 502
Columbia, MO 65205 USA
E-mail: sab@socketis.net
Books on and from South Asia

Education About Asia magazine
Association for Asian Studies
1021 East Huron St.
Ann Arbor, MI 48104
Ph: 734-665-2490
E-mail: postmaster@aasianst.org

West Music
P.O. Box 5521
1208 5th St.
Coralville, IA 52241
Ph: 800-397-9378
Source of multicultural books, tapes, and instruments

Note: Also try the excellent Asian outreach and resource centers at universities strong in Asian studies. Contact AskAsia for current addresses.

Internet Sites

AccessAsia: Many web links organized by country and category
http://www.accessasia.com.

Asia-Pacific Magazine online
http://coombs.anu.edu.au/asia-pacific-magazine

India Online: Resource links on India
http://indiaonline.com/

Indiana University East Asia Studies Center
http://www.easc.indiana.edu

Internet Guide to Buddhism and Buddhist Studies
URL http://www.ciolek.com/WWWVL-Buddhism.html

Korea Web Weekly; many listings about Korea
http://www.kimsoft.com/korea.htm

List of Internet sites dealing with Greater China (i.e., PR China, Tibet, Taiwan, Hong Kong, Macau, Singapore)
URL http://www.univie.ac.at/Sinologie/netguide.htm

Material on Aung San Suu Kyi and the struggle to free Burma
http://sunsite.unc.edu/freeburma/index.html

National Clearinghouse on U.S.-Japan Studies
http://www.indiana.edu./~japan/

Newslink: Great way to find many Asian newspapers and journals
http://www.newslink.org/nonusa.html

Pacific Bridge Arts: Links on Asian arts
http://www.pacific-bridge-arts.com/

Sawnet: Resources on South Asian women
http://www.umiacs.umd.edu/users/sawweb/sawnet/news.html

The Islam Page with resources about Islam
http://www.islamworld.net

Southeast Asia Web: Rich resources on Southesat Asia
http://www.gunung.com/seasiaweb/

More lists of sites on Southesat Asia
http://www.bangkoknet.com/indochina

Fine site of Sackler/Freer Asian art museums
http://www.si.edu/asia/